LIL BABY 4

SA'ID SALAAM

Urban Aesop Publications

Email: saidmsalaam@gmail.com

Proofreader: Tiffany Thomas-Huff

Cover Art: Sa'id Salaam

DEDICATION

To us

CHAPTER ONE

"She was a pillar of her community! A rock! A philanthropist..." the preacher preached. Actually he read from the script since he was paid to do so. Big Mama knew this day would have to come so she took the liberty of writing her own eulogy.

She had a feeling hers could be a closed casket affair so she took the liberty of having a photoshoot for the picture standing next to that closed casket. Sugar Bear had to have the lid closed on her send off so her grandson returned the favor.

Lil Baby missed most of what was said from the pulpit but didn't miss much since it was all bull shit. The woman in the box had caused so much misery and so many funerals they should have a parade. The church was packed by friends and foes. Some would miss her, others happy to see her go.

Meanwhile, memories of the old woman's proverbs floated around in her head. She finally understood 'seeing a man about a mule', but had no idea if 'fat meat was greasy' as the woman used to ask. Either way she had a lifetime of euphemisms and sayings to guide her even after her demise.

Most of the family was in attendance but most weren't mourning. They were more concerned with what happened next since they still had to eat. Life is for the living so fuck the dead bitch in the box. Fitting sentiments since Big Mama didn't care much about them either in life.

Ethyl missed most of what was said as well since she was consumed with her own thoughts. Mainly, what came next. After a lifetime of crime and corruption she didn't know what happened now. It was all she knew and it was all snatched in a flurry of gunshots. Her eyes rolled over to the angry teen seated next to her.

'Tuh' Ethyl huffed at the so-called heir to the throne. No one said it out loud but this was Lil Baby's fault. She was literally sleeping with the enemy and gave the assassin a way in. She was not ready and probably never would be.

Then, there were the millions they had earned over the years. Including the years before this child came along. Ethyl 'tuh-ed' another 'tuh' in her head at the girl having any claim to it. No, she cut throats, lied, cheated and stole for that money and had more right to it than anyone. Which was exactly what Beatrice was thinking on the other side of her.

'Hmp!' Beatrice huffed inwardly at the notion of anyone other than her deserving what her mother left behind. She was her only direct descendant and the millions belonged to her. Sure, she would break Ethyl off a lil 'sum for her years of faithful service. Of course she would look after her beloved nieces and make sure they were straight for life.

"Now, if we can get you to line up and say a word or two..." the pastor pastored when he reached the end of his script. He felt a strong need to gargle with holy water after all the lies he just told. He read all the warm and fuzzy things Big Mama wrote about herself but the truth was, the world was a better place without her.

The throngs of attendees complied and filed out by pews to say a final word to the woman in the box. They would have to speak up a little to be heard through the lid because Rue made sure they would have to keep her casket closed. Big Mama was smiling in the picture but was a mess inside the box.

The mourners gave condolences to the daughter and granddaughters before saying what they had to say. Detective Larue gave a respectful nod towards the family but was met by blank stares and scowls. She fought off a smirk and took her turn at the casket.

"I win you dirty, blood sucking, murderous bitch. You got what you had coming. Now reap those seeds you sowed in hell..." she whispered and came up with a refreshed smile. It wouldn't be final until the woman was in the ground and covered with dirt. So she headed out to her car to be the first out at the gravesite.

"I guess I'll go first," Ethyl sighed when the line came to an end. She stood and smoothed her dress before stepping forward. She looked around then leaned in to say what was on her heart. "Where is the cash? I'ma let yo kin keep the stores and car wash. I just need that bread baby."

2

Anyone watching, and plenty were, would assume she was summing up over fifty years of friendship. The truth was she needed to know where the stash of cash was. Big Mama included her in almost everything except what she did with the millions of dollars in profits.

The Family funneled plenty of cash into legit and semi legit businesses. They owned barbershops, beauty salons, car washes and car lots. Not to mention corner stores on corners in every ward in the city. Slews of houses used as trap houses or rental properties as well. Still there were millions of dollars in cash that couldn't go in any bank. The search was on to find it.

"Gurl..." Ethyl sighed and shook her head. "We been through some shit ain't we? But we got through it, mmhm we did. Ion know how we 'sposed to get through this one though. You always had me to run shit by but who I got? Not that goofy gal who let our opp in the house. Guess we lucky he ain't kill us all. Well, I'ma need that bread tho baby..."

"Hey grammaw," Lil Baby began when it was finally her turn. She was the last born so it was only fair she got the last word. Her mind scrambled for words that wouldn't come. Sure she planned to avenge her just like Rue avenged his own granny. She wasn't even mad at him anymore since she now felt what he felt one hundred percent. The burning rage and desire for get back, no matter the cost. If someone could bottle vengeance it could fuel the entire world. "Yeah, I'll see you when I get there."

~

"Hmmmm," Buella hummed as she arrived at the gravesite. She had arrived early enough to attend the church service but couldn't bring herself to go inside. She had been to far too many funerals already and couldn't stomach another. Her heart nearly stopped when she realized the stunning young lady dipped in black, designer labels was her baby sister.

She was the only reason she was here. To save her sister before this city put her in a hole in the ground as well. New Orleans had claimed her mother, father, sister, girlfriend and now grandmother. The sinister city nearly claimed her and caused her hand to rub the remnants of the scar that remained from being chained up in the swamp house. It was a reminder of how close she came to being stretched out in a fancy casket.

Faces lit with recognition as she made her way through the mourners. She returned nods but didn't speak until coming face to face with the gloating detective. Larue nodded her greeting to the young woman as she passed.

"Fuck you," Buella replied to the nod and kept on going. She wasn't late since she didn't want to hear some preacher lying about what a good person Big Mama was. Her grandmother was the devil and she wanted to, need to, see that box covered with dirt.

Lil Baby was locked in on the pretty casket. It twisted her face with the contradiction of spending twenty thousand dollars to bury in the dirt. Big Mama took the liberty of designing her own casket and whole funeral. Her wishes were carried out in death just as they were in life. Buella furrowed her brow at the young woman locked in on her as she approached.

"Is that..." Alexis asked when she spotted the familiar face approaching. She hadn't seen the girl in person but there were enough pictures in Big Mama's house to make the identification. Plus she looked so much like the grieving teen at her side.

"Buella?" Lil Baby asked and blinked to make sure her eyes weren't lying to her. The flutter in her heart turned into a smile that never made it to her face.

"Hey Agatha," Buella greeted. The smile in her heart didn't make it to her face either but she was happy to see her baby sister again. "You look good!"

"Tuh!" Lil Baby huffed in indignation. "Now you show up? You couldn't show up when your sister got kilt tho!"

"I ain't come here for her..." Buella said and nodded towards the casket. "I came here for you!"

"For me? For what?" Lil Baby reeled.

"To come to Atlanta with me. I got a good job. A nice apartment. I can get you into my old school..." she laid out like a red carpet. Buella went as hard in life as she did in the street and got her degree in criminal justice. She knew she owed for her contribution to the misery and intended to pay her debt.

"You should go," Alexis spoke out of turn but it had to be said. Buella tilted her head curiously at the intrusion.

"This family business, if you don't mind," Buella spat as nicely as one can with their fist balled up. Something about just being in New Orleans made her angry and she was ready to leave.

"She is family! This is Alexis, our sister. We got the same daddy," Lil Baby explained. Buella gave the girl a once over and saw the truth etched in the girl's face. She nodded at their shared father's face on the girl's head. That's all she had coming though so she turned back to her baby sister.

"Girl, come to Atlanta! All this drama is finally over!" Buella pleaded. She followed the recent events online even before the graduation party massacre made national news.

Lil Baby saw the sincerity in her eyes and knew no one loved her like this young woman did. She looked over at their aunt Beatrice as she plotted and planned. She knew her mother left millions somewhere and she wanted it. As if she were most entitled to it.

Lil Baby looked over at Ethyl who stared off at something. Whatever it was made her eyes twinkle. After a lifetime of being a sidekick she could finally run this city herself. She literally swooned under the sudden intoxication of power. She too knew of the millions but Big Mama hadn't told her where it was all tucked and stashed since she hadn't planned on leaving so suddenly.

Lil Baby's lips twisted at the baby in her belly and the man who put it there. Rue was out there moving freely since he cut off the head of the notorious Big Mama and dismantled her Family. She looked to Alexis who nodded with her opinion for her to go. She inhaled, exhaled and made her decision.

"I ain't going nowhere!" she announced triumphantly. "The drama ain't over. It's just getting started...."

"That's what I'm afraid of," Buella sighed. "I'll be in town until Monday. I'm hoping, praying you will come with me?"

"Don't hole yo breath," Lil Baby pouted and turned her head to signal she was done talking. So was the preacher and the funeral came to an end.

Detective Larue stayed after all the mourners left. She didn't move until the final crumb of dirt was packed over the grave. She hawked up a good spit and spat on her grave.

CHAPTER TWO

"This ain't right..." Toddy moaned as Bee popped the lock to the funeral home.

"Ion care if it's right, left, up or muhfucking down! I was told to do it and I'm finna do it!" Bee shot back as the lock gave way.

"Mannnn," Toddy sighed and followed him inside. Now came the grim task of searching for what they came for. Better yet, who they came for.

"Nope," Bee said as the first casket contained an older man. Next an older woman but they struck paydirt on the third. "Here she go."

"Dang!" Bee reeled and winced at the hole in the pretty woman's head. Even in death Jazzy-belle was a jazzy broad. She had plenty of relatives but no family so no one had come to collect her shell. She was due to be incinerated soon but wouldn't be around when her turn came.

"Let's bag the bitch so we can get up out of her..." Toddy ordered and searched for a body bag. He grabbed her still manicured feet as Toddy grabbed her upper body. Together they lifted her out the box and into the bag. They left the same way they came and put the body in the trunk. Then drove where they were told to drive and parked the car.

"Who's supposed to take it from here?" Toddy asked but Bee couldn't answer even if he wanted to. His orders came from Tony who was now the highest ranking man left in the family. They watched behind them as they pulled away after changing cars.

Lil Baby watched them watching and waited until they were out of sight before getting into the car. She wanted the corpse put in the front

7

seat so she could talk to it on the long ride out to New Iberia. Tony shut that risky request down and had her placed in the trunk. It would have been hard to explain a stolen corpse in the passenger seat if she got pulled over by the cops. Especially with the modified Draco in the backseat. Lil Baby had to just talk to herself on the ride out to the swamp.

"Ump!" she grunted when it came time to pull the dead weight from the trunk. Fueled by anger and a tinge of lunacy made it easier to drag the body bag into the house.

"Where you at Bella?" she called out into the darkness of the swamp after opening the sliding glass door to nowhere. Bullfrogs and other creatures hollered back as she stepped back over to the bag containing the remains.

"Look at you now. With a hole in yo head," she teased as she pulled the bag away from Jazzy-belle's naked frame. She looked the dead body over with a morbid curiosity. Her eyes blinked in the finality of death before her shoulders shrugged and it was time to do what she had come for.

"Time to go..." Lil Baby sang as she rolled the body over to the edge. She had no idea of the impending cremation but was determined the woman didn't get a proper send off. She had sprang to bury Patty-cake and her baby while Ethyl made the arrangements for Juice and the other fallen soldiers. A lot of funerals but Jazzy-belle wouldn't get one.

The body landed with a splash but none of the usual splashing of feeding time. It sank quickly to the bottom of the blackish water where it would be claimed by the gators. Lil Baby slid the door closed but didn't lock it since she planned to return very soon. The night was young and she still had something left on her to do list.

The ride back to the city passed rather quickly since her mind was consumed with murder. Killing Rue was top priority and took her mind off her other problem. One she couldn't ignore for long since it would only get worse. She knew what needed to be done, now she had to do it.

～

Meanwhile Rue alternated between watching the security camera feed on the monitor and the chick with most of his dick in her mouth. The soft gags stole his attention when he reached her larynx. He was as hard as he was going to get so he pulled up on the bed and flipped her onto her side.

"Oooh!" Choo-choo giggled when he lifted her leg and pushed

8

inside of her from the side. He lifted her leg onto his shoulder so he could run his whole dick into the hot juice box.

"Shit..." Rue gushed at the sight and feel of slipping in and out of the soaked snatch. Choo-choo wasn't very smart and definitely wasn't loyal but the girl had some good pussy. And that's plenty if that's all you have to offer. He was so busy watching her coat his dick in creamy goodness that he forgot about watching the footage from the camera outside of his house. He was about to miss the show.

"Just point, and spray..." Lil Baby repeated the instructions she received on the modified machine gun. It was designed to shoot semi automatic but the gunsmith on payroll made it spit fully automatic. It would empty the fifty round clip in seconds so it was good another was taped to the bottom. She grabbed two more connected clips and got out of the car.

She knew Rue favored the fifty five inch TV mounted on his bedroom wall over the hundred inch TV in the living room. She knew because she had gotten pregnant in front of it one of the nights she spent there with him.

The directions repeated in her head when she got around to the back of the house. The cameras there picked her up as well but Choo-choo had just come all over Rue's dick so he wasn't watching. Not until she said 'just point, and spray' sending the first fifty rounds into the house. The windows shattered under the barrage of bullets that went straight through the walls as well. They tore through the new comforter set and pillows she recently bought him. The gunfire lit up the night in bright orange and stole Rue away from watching the quivering pussy contracting on his dick. Luckily for him and her he was watching from another house up the street.

"Dang lil mama!" Rue laughed when Lil Baby on screen flipped the clip and began firing again. One of the bullets caught the gas line and began filling the house with fumes. She swapped the spent clips for two more and sent another hundred rounds into the house. One caused the spark that caused the explosion that blew out the rest of the windows.

"Burn in hell bitch!" she spat as the gun clicked empty. Then walked casually to her car to drive home. She needed some rest since she had some more killing to do in the morning.

"It's like that huh..." Rue snarled after remotely watching the murder attempt. He had hoped she would understand and she did. He hoped she could get past it and she would. It would just be over his dead body. He switched back to Choo-choo's tonsil and fucked her face until he skeeted down her throat. They cuddled up like a couple and drifted off to sleep.

~

"**W**ell this is some real bullshit..." Lil Baby groaned as she got dressed. She looked at her outfit in the mirror. It looked good but she knew it wouldn't fit in a few months if she didn't get a move on it.

The well appointed house was eerily quiet and empty since Big Mama moved to the graveyard. Ethyl had a nice loft downtown but always stayed at the house with them. She hadn't been back since the funeral. The usual contingent of security men was reduced to a couple killers.

"Mawnin Miss Lil Baby," Toddy greeted even though he was ten years older than the teen. Bee popped up behind him, ready to follow her wherever she went. Except she didn't want to be followed this morning.

"Y'all stay here!" she ordered and popped the locks on the car. It suddenly got old to her and she decided she needed a new one. After all she had been through she deserved it.

The security men looked at each other, trying to figure out which orders to follow. On one hand Tony demanded they stay on her ass wherever she went. Now she just shouted them down and demanded they stay. She had pulled off the block by the time their shoulders shrugged and they went back inside.

Lil Baby was on autopilot and didn't register the banal banter on the radio. She didn't miss anything since the DJs weren't talking about much. Other than making fun of entertainers who were doing way better in life than they were. The biggest critics are the people who don't do or have shit. Somehow they carved out a market in making fun of people. The world got weirder by the day.

"Tuh!" Lil Baby huffed indignantly when she passed the street that would have taken her to the bootleg doctor who performed Patty-cake's abortion. She wouldn't take those chances with her own life and limbs so she booked an appointment at the real clinic.

"Agatha Fontenot," she explained and showed her ID to get into the secured building.

"Check in with the desk and take a number," the man replied after checking the name against the names on his list. His long list of women and girls terminating unwanted or unsafe pregnancies.

Lil Baby looked straight ahead and followed directions. She felt some kind of way when she had to take a number like Big Mama used to do at the butcher shop. Now she was in funk while waiting her turn in the stirrups.

"Fontenot..." Dr Monique Johnson reeled when she read the next name on her list. She was relieved it wasn't the Buella girl she had seen several times. A heavy sigh escaped her throat when she thought about when Buella's sister Bella had come through as well. A few months later she was on the news as one of the city's many homicides. Another thought twisted her face when she remembered Buella saying she had two sisters. She snatched the file and marched into the procedure room. "Agatha Fontenot?"

"Yes," Lil Baby replied and saw the woman's heart break in her eyes. The same eyes that instantly saw her older sister's face in her face.

"I um," she stammered and sighed since she had a job to do and service to provide. Neither of them were minding other people's business.

"Are you ok?" Lil Baby asked softly since the woman looked so sad.

"Me? Uh, yes. I'm here to perform your procedure..." she said after shaking off the shock. The patient had been prepped so she got down to the business that paid her.

"Is your ride ready?" the doctor asked when she wrapped it up.

"No, I drove myself. I'm good," she replied.

"Except state law says you're not good. I'll call your sister," the doctor sighed. She took a final look at the baby faced young woman and shook her head.

Lil Baby twisted her lips at the scorn she perceived but it wasn't that. It just broke the doctor's heart to service sisters, mothers and grandmothers. Some procedures were necessary for so many reasons. While others were just reckless and used abortion as birth control. Agatha took the same place in the waiting room and waited for Alexis to come pick her up.

"Hey dere," her sister called down to her while she scrolled through her news feed.

"Hey I..." Lil Baby began to give Alexis the spiel she had practiced. She had warned her about having unprotected sex but she did it anyway. Except it was Buella looking down at her. She popped up to her feet quicker than a boxer after a flash knockdown. Except she didn't want to fight. Instead she slammed into her sister and had a good cry.

A great cry actually since she had kept everything bottled up for so long. This was the cry she missed when her father abused her. It was for her mother dying with a needle in her arm. This cry was for Patty-cake and her baby. For Juice and the other fallen soldiers. She shed more tears for her grandmother and finally for the sister holding her so tightly.

"You left me!" Lil Baby wailed and tried to pull away.

"No, I ran for my life!" Buella shot back and held her firm. Her sister struggled for a moment, then went limp and melted back into her arms. The doctor shed a tear from the hallway. She hoped for a happily ever after for the Fontenot sisters but Lil Baby was right when she told her sister that the drama was just beginning.

CHAPTER THREE

"I don't miss this part one bit!" Buella said as she watched the two security guards posted up near their table. Both Toddy and Bee had their guns on their laps under the table as they sat at the next table.

"It is what it is," Lil Baby shrugged since she was used to it. She glanced towards the door every few seconds like someone on the run. Which allowed her to see her other sister when she entered the restaurant. "Here she come. Be nice!"

"I'm always nice," Buella shot back and pasted a wide, fake smile on her face. Lil Baby just shook her head and cracked up.

"Hey dere sis," Alexis challenged and cocked her head at Buella. She felt some kind of way after being snubbed at the funeral.

"Yeah, she one of us," Buella laughed as their shared father's features stuck out plain as day. Luckily their father was a handsome man so it didn't hurt.

"Buella meet Alexis. Alexis, Buella..." Lil Baby formally introduced. She cheesed broadly at the prospect of family since they were all she had left.

Lil Baby missed most of the introductory banter as her sisters asked and answered about each other and themselves. Her eyes pulled back to the door once again on the lookout. Rue was out there and she couldn't rest until he was put to rest. A dirt nap that is because this couldn't end any other way. One or both of them would be dead before this story could end.

"Agatha?" Buella asked for a third time and got the girl's attention.

"Why are you calling me by my 'guvment name?" she laughed and tuned in.

"Cuz she called you Lil Baby fifty-eleven times and you ain't answer!" Alexis chimed in on behalf of her other younger sister.

"What! Dang!" Lil Baby squealed playfully. She was enjoying being the baby sister once again. Being Lil Baby the baby sister sure beat pimping and dealing.

"I said, come to Atlanta with me!" Buella pleaded once more. She witnessed her own head turn to the new sister and invited her too. "You can come too!"

"Me?" Alexis reeled and cheesed broadly at being included. She too had to settle for seconds with chicks like Nicki instead of sisters. She now had sisters. "I got a kid! And my customers..."

"She is the baddest bitch in the city when it comes to doing hair!" Lil Baby proclaimed.

"And she would make even more bread in a bigger city like Atlanta!" Buella assured. She sang the praises of the city like she was on the Atlanta tourism board. Lil Baby smiled along with them but had no intentions on going anywhere. Not until it was done. Not until she exacted her revenge. She was glad to see a distraction walk through the door.

"We will finish this later," she interjected as Choo-choo neared the table. "Hey gurl?"

"Hey y'all!" Choo-choo cheered and hugged her neck with Rue's DNA sloshing around inside her. "I saw you post you were here..."

"Come on and sit. We just chopping it up," Lil Baby insisted since the subject would have to change. Which was exactly what she wanted since she didn't want to keep talking about moving.

"Chile, why are you posting your whereabouts?" Alexis fussed. She witnessed their grandmother get killed as well and knew this wasn't safe. Posting her whereabouts was bait and she hoped Rue would bite.

"Cuz..." she shot back and cocked her head like she wished a nigga would. She had a nine millimeter in her purse in case he did.

Not that he would make it past the men posted up outside or the two more sitting at the next table. Rue killed Jazzy-belle and Big Mama in front of a bunch of people but they were street people so that information never made it to the cops. The case was closed with Jazzy-belle being the culprit since she had a list of bodies up and down the Mississippi river.

"We'll pick this up later. I only have a few more days in town," Buella sighed and stood.

"Ok gurl!" Lil Baby stood as well and hugged her neck. She stepped back proudly and watched her two older sisters hug. A tear fell for the one who wasn't here and her heart ached for Bella.

"Nice to meet you," Alexis sang. She was looking forward to seeing her again before she left the city. In the meanwhile she was contemplating the relocation offer. It would mean starting over but sometimes starting over is the best thing a person can do.

~

The girls were yacking it up and having a good time while a more serious conversation was taking place nearby. Big Mama owned a small restaurant in the French quarter which was a fitting place to discuss the weighty matters.

"Hey there auntie," Beatrice sang and hugged Ethyl's neck when she stood. She arrived half an hour before their meeting out of habit and found the older woman was already there.

"Hey ya self beautiful!" Ethyl gushed at the jet black woman's features. Her smooth black skin served as the perfect canvas for the sharp nose and thick lips that gave her an exotic beauty. The niceties were over so they sank to their seats and got down to business.

"That chile can't run no Family!" Ethyl put it bluntly. Beatrice nodded appreciatively at her bluntness and decided to return the favor.

"Look, Ion care nothing about y'all business. I don't. I never did," she admitted. "But my mama left behind some money and I need that. I'm her heir. Me!"

"You is. No doubt about that," Ethyl nodded and agreed. "But I helped build it. Half of err penny got my name on it! I'm the one who was out chere in these streets. Taking penitentiary chances to get this money. So don't come in here thinking you finna run off with the cake!"

"Hmp..." Beatrice grunted. The woman had no interest in the business and never took part. She had plenty of her own money but money never stopped anyone from being greedy. "I can go half."

"And take care of yo niece out yo half," Ethyl pouted. She loved Lil Baby but loved money just a little more. Plus the power to move men was intoxicating. She was tipsy now with Tony and three more shooters posted in and around the joint.

"Naw, she ain't got nothing coming out my half. I put in work myself! Too much work..." Beatrice shot back. Her face contorted when the memories came rushing back into her head. First Clarence creeped into her room every time her mother left the house. Running a criminal organization was lots of work so the woman was always out of the house. That gave the predator all the time he needed with his prey.

When she was at cheer practice or dance team he would take it out on her brother. Charles in turn returned the favor and abused Beatrice as well. They were taking her body in the house so she gladly gave it away for free in the streets. Until she went viral enough to catch the attention of producers out west. They flew her to LA and pumped drugs and dicks into her and made her famous. Rich and famous but she still wanted the fortune her mother left behind.

"Hell naw, I earned it. And I want what I got coming!" she decided with a deep scowl.

"And you finna get it," Ethyl assured. "Now, where yo mama put the legit money?"

"Are you asking me?" Beatrice laughed. Had she known where the money was she and it would have been gone. "Ion care nothing about what y'all got going on in the street but I want my inheritance!"

"Hmp..." the woman huffed again. She was set to meet with the lawyer on Monday to shed some light on the legitimate enterprises. In the meanwhile it was business as usual on the streets.

"Guess I'll see you Monday at uncle Clyde's office," Beatrice chuckled. She knew the reading of the will would go her way. After all, she was the closest heir to the throne.

"Monday," Ethyl nodded and watched her stand. All eyes watched the bubble butt bouncing under the short, leather, mini skirt as she left the building. Another nod of her head brought Tony to her side.

"What we looking like?" he asked since he had a vested interest in the outcome. Ethyl assumed the throne and now called the shots.

"Finna see..." she sighed and looked in the direction the woman just departed. "You may need to make a decision. You gone have to pick a team soon."

"Ain't no picking. We finna keep doing what we been doing," he replied instantly. It now made sense that it was Rue who was hitting their spots. He was atop the things to do list and needed to be done as soon as possible.

"Any word on that boy?" Ethyl asked since her mind was on the same page. They couldn't flip to the next page until Rue got flipped himself.

"Naw, but money moves thangs. Someone finna say something," he assured.

"Well, double that. Two hundred grand for his ass!" she ordered. "But, he's gotta be alive. Still a buck to put a bullet in his head."

"Check," Tony agreed. He was the man next to the man next to the woman. Now he answered directly to the woman in charge. Lil Baby had been the heir apparent until her breach of protocol brought the kingdom down. It was she who got the killer close enough to kill Big Mama.

"For now keep err thang the same," she ordered.

"Same cut?" Tony immediately asked. By his estimation he should be getting a larger cut since the queen was dead.

"Hell yeah! Her granddaughter get her share!" she shot back with enough gumption to make it seem true. She had no intention of increasing Lil Baby's share of anything. This was her exit plan and the kid would have to get it like they did. Out the mud.

"Hmp, ok den," Tony said from his throat but the words didn't reach his heart. She was right about one thing, he did need to pick a side. And he did.

Tony's eyes shifted along with Ethyl's round back side as she left the establishment. His head shook at how fine she once was even though she was keeping it pretty tight nearing sixty. Her new security guard followed behind her since she outsourced the job. He looked over to his own men and stood.

"Y'all go on home now. I'm finna go lay some pipe," he ordered and walked out. Laying some pipe sounded like a good idea so they went home to do the same. Tony's mind twisted, shimmied and shook as he weighed his options. His head nodded with his decision. "I'm on my damn team..."

CHAPTER FOUR

"Hmp?" Rue asked and tilted his head curiously at the picture on his screen. Lil Baby was still kind of shy so the bare breast was as much of a picture he could get out of her. It was a pretty, firm, yellow titty so he used it as her contact picture. He hadn't changed his number but she hadn't called since he murdered her grandmother. That curiosity got the best of him so he took the call. "Hello?"

"Hello? Hmp. This nigga kills my folk and ask me hello," she fussed and sighed heavily through the line. Rue held his tongue since it was what it was. He tried to let it go but when the opportunity popped up he took it. He tried to resist it but couldn't.

"I'm saying tho..." he shrugged.

"Saying what! Huh! Why you do that shit!" Lil Baby growled. "Everything was going good. Why you ain't let it go? For me..."

"I tried to. Swear 'fo God I tried," he said and exhaled heavily. "On God I tried, but..."

"But what?" Lil Baby practically pleaded. She hoped he would explain something that would make things like they used to be. "Why you have to do it? We were good. Wasn't I enough?"

"I tried," he sighed. It wasn't the answer that perturbed her, it was the shrug she could feel through the line.

"I tried too," she sighed and shrugged as well. "I put a hundred rounds in yo raggedy house and still missed."

"We really finna play that game?" Rue dared. He understood and expected her to strike back. But wondered if she would take it far enough for him to have to kill her.

"Ain't no game and ain't no one playing! It's on sight nigga!" she shot back and hung up.

"So be it," Rue said into the empty line and tossed the phone aside. The security light outside popped on when the motion detector detected some motion.

Rue reached for one of the many guns strewn about and headed for the door just as the intruder reached it. A glance at the security monitor showed Tony approaching with his own gun dangling from his side. Rue could have easily put a few rounds through the door and knocked the man back into the street. Instead he smiled and pulled the door open.

"Sup woadie..." Rue greeted and showed off his new gold grill. He could now spend some of the booty he acquired from raiding the Family's business.

"Sup says the man with the two hundred on his head," Tony laughed and looked around as he entered. It was a dangerous game playing both sides but also filled both sides of his pockets.

"Shit we seeing that much err day!" Rue laughed and reminded him of his worth. While Rue, Ethyl and Lil Baby were concerned with revenge he was only concerned with the money. And Rue was a natural born dope boy who doubled profits. His heavy hand prevented anyone from running off or sticking them up.

"And you the MVP lil buddy!" Tony laughed. The neat stacks of cash on the table made him giddy. Especially since he was underreporting proceeds to Ethyl.

"So what we finna do?" Rue asked as he began bagging the cash.

"About what?" Tony needed to know since he had lost his train of thought trying to count the bundles of bread as they went into the bag.

"About them broads. That old bitch put a ticket on my head and the lil one done shot up crib!" he protested.

"Yeah..." Tony sighed since he didn't have a good answer. He had an answer, it just wasn't good.

"Hmp," Rue huffed since he knew the answer too.

"Chances are they might get this bread and go 'bout they business," Tony said hopefully. He had no hopes of getting anything when the will was read but hoped it would be enough to placate the women and leave the street shit to the menfolk.

"Let's hope..." Rue hoped as well since he didn't want to have to kill Lil Baby. He would though...

$\sim$

"**M**awnin..." Ethyl greeted when Beatrice joined her in the waiting room of the attorney's office. She had been there for an hour already in hopes of having a word with the lawyer before anyone else arrived. She had a bundle of cash next to the pistol in her purse hoping to persuade him one way or the other. Not to mention no panties since pussy can be persuasive too. He hadn't arrived yet so that plan died when the heirs began to arrive.

"Miss Ethyl," Beatrice nodded casually since her mind had changed about giving the woman anything she might have had coming.

"Hmp, so be it," the older woman replied. She didn't have to read her mind since it was written all over her face. She had hoped this would be amicable but would gladly get on the fuck shit if it came down to it.

"Good morning..." Buella sighed as she entered the office. She didn't want to be here but wasn't going to turn anything down. She nearly died for it herself and felt like she deserved it. Her vehicle was gassed up and ready to hit the road once this was over. She had spent the weekend trying to convince Lil Baby to come to Atlanta with her and still had hopes she would. Reading the will was closure and maybe it would open a new chapter for the Fontenot sisters.

"Good morning," the two women replied in unison. The door opened and all heads turned. All expectations were dashed when Mr Clyde Walker walked in instead of Lil Baby.

"Good morning. Is everyone here?" he asked and looked the women over. Beatrice's thick thighs demanded a pause before moving along.

"Good morning," they all replied like a chorus but Beatrice took the lead.

"Everyone except for Agatha. We don't have to wait tho," she said on behalf of all.

"Hmp?" the attorney hummed and furrowed his brow. A moment later a smirk appeared and nodded his head. "Sure. Step into my office..."

Beatrice never let an opportunity pass so she put on a dazzling display as she walked by the man holding the door open for the women. He was a man so she slung her ample ass cheeks from side to side as she entered. The attorney nodded again in appreciation since who doesn't appreciate a nice fat ass.

"Ok then," he began once they were all seated. He reached for the button that started the recording of the session and got down to business. "We are here for the reading of the will for Miss Eleanor Fontenot..."

All heads turned when he pointed a remote control towards the large TV on the wall. Moments later the late, great Big Mama appeared on the screen. She held up a newspaper to verify the date and to her people's astonishment it was dated two weeks prior.

"Miss Fontenot was in the habit of refreshing her wishes from time to time," he explained. In truth the woman changed her will often when in her feelings about one thing or another. Heads turned from him back to the video when Big Mama cleared her throat and began to speak.

"Hey y'all," Big Mama greeted with a chuckle. She was amused by the shock faces she imagined but the weight of the occasion quickly settled on her neck. "Well, if y'all all here then someone must have got my ass. If I was a betting woman I'd guess it was one of my own. Juice is loyal but sloppy at times. He wouldn't do it tho. Ethyl, maybe? I seen that twinkle in yo eye a few times. You was loyal but wanted to be me.

My darling daughter Beatrice. I love you baby..."

"I love you too mama!" Beatrice squealed and blew a kiss as her mother continued.

"My grand babies, Buella and Agatha. Y'all know y'all granny loves you guys. I love you all, that's why y'all in the room. Guess I better get down to why we here. To find out who gets my shit.

The main house goes to Beatrice. You grew up in it so it's only right. I know it holds some bad memories, so make some good ones. Settle down and make you some babies. Raise them better than I did with you and your brother.

My best friend, my sister, my right hand bitch Ethyl Lafontaine!" Big Mama smiled and laughed. Only a trace of mirth remained when she continued. "You've been getting yours off the top for as long as I can remember. Sure I knew about your lil skimming. The condo you bought on the water. The secret accounts you put all you pinched over the years. I have to respect it because it kept you close. Kept you on your grind since the more money I made the more you could take. Enjoy it, cuz it's all you got coming.

Look at you, lip poked out like someone did you something. Gurl you are still straight and alive so be happy! My darling Buella. Not sure if you are here or not? Ain't come to your own sister's funeral. Just missed Agatha's graduation. You spoiled and that's just trifling! All you worried about is yo self. That's why I ain't left you shit. I had a stick of bubble gum for you, but I ate it..." Big Mama paused long enough to blow a bubble from that gum before going on.

"Now, speaking of Agatha. Where is she?" she snickered and pretended to look around the room. If she could see into the room she would have seen the sour faces. She must have known it too and let go of a cackle.

"Yeah, I'ma head out..." Buella said when she had enough. She stood to leave and no one tried to stop her or call her back. Ethyl was still stuck and Beatrice needed to hear this until the end.

"Anyways, y'all tell my Lil Baby grammaw loves her like a fat kid loves cake! Love her enough to pay her way through college. And once she is done she can come back and see Mr Walker. See 'ifn there's anything else coming..." Big Mama on the screen concluded.

"And there we have it," Mr Walker sighed and waited for what he knew was coming.

"Oh hell naw!" Beatrice shouted as she hopped to her feet. Ethyl felt the same but waited her turn.

"What's wrong Miss Fontenot?" he asked as if he didn't understand. He did but was a good actor after disappointing people for decades.

"Where is the money at? I know my granny was holding some millions!" Beatrice demanded and scanned the office like it might be somewhere in the room.

"At least ten by my estimation," Ethyl tossed in like skeeting lighter fluid on burning charcoal.

"Not even close!" the lawyer shot back indignantly. "Cut that figure in half through the laundry..."

He began since turning dirty bread into clean cash came with a premium cost. Laundering money was big business and a crime in itself. Which is why the banks and bankers who did the dastardly deeds charged up to sixty percent.

"So, five million then!" Beatrice countered without missing a beat.

"Which she spent lavishly in life. Now, her accountant can give you a better picture of her spendings. All I know is what she put in the will..." he sighed.

Both women sat in a silent simmer like a good soup. A low boil, trying to figure out who to take their anger out on. Beatrice thought about attacking the lawyer. He had her by a few inches but she thought she could whoop him if she got the jump on him. Her head slowly turned towards Ethyl as she replayed her mother's words.

"So, where is this money you skimmed from my mama?" she demanded and thought about jumping on her now.

"Let me see..." Ethyl said as she rummaged through her purse. "Nope, ain't nothing in here 'cept my razor..."

"Uh, ladies," Mr Walker interjected. Not that he cared what they did, just where they did it. As in, not in his office.

"What!" both turned and snapped.

"I have another appointment," he explained.

"Whatever!" they shouted together and stormed out.

"I'll be to see you," Beatrice warned as they left the building.

"And I'll be waiting!"she laughed and hopped into the new Benz she bought for her new role. It was her turn to run this city.

CHAPTER FIVE

"**B**uella here..." Alexis announced when she saw the rental car barreling into the yard. The old security men would have surrounded it with guns drawn but the new ones just peeked from the window of the security house.

"Here we go..." Lil Baby said and rolled her eyes when she heard her sister's angry steps as she ascended the stairs.

"Girl, why didn't you come to the office!" Buella asked. She was content with the will since she got exactly what she wanted. Nothing, since she didn't want a penny of the dirty money.

"Cuz..." she sighed since she didn't have an answer. She preferred having the old lady back instead of divvying up her assets.

"Cuz, ain't no answer!" both older sisters in the room shot back.

"So, what did she leave err body?" Alexis wanted to know. Big Mama took some care for her when she was growing up so she wondered if she left her anything in the will.

"Err body?" Buella laughed since not everybody got anything. In fact she didn't get a coin, pot nor piss. "Shit, that old bitch ain't leave us shit! Say Ethyl was skimming so she ain't leave her nuffin either. I..."

"What the hell?" Lil Baby interrupted and hopped to her feet. She rushed out to confront the woman getting out of her car in the driveway since Toddy and Bee hadn't budged. They saw a woman and went back to their video game since they were too new to know women were just as dangerous as men. The stranger went into her trunk just as the Fontenot sisters arrived at her side.

"What the hell is you doing?" Alexis demanded and stepped in front

25

of Lil Baby. Buella took tacit note of how she put herself between her and their little sister.

"Uh, my job," she hissed and resumed pulling the item from the trunk. She wasn't an assassin so it wasn't a shotgun. She was in fact a real estate agent so she produced a 'for sale' sign.

"The fuck is you doing?" Lil Baby growled and moved on the woman as she tried to post the signs.

"Wait!" Buella shouted and stepped in before Lil Baby could tackle the woman.

"Wait what? This bitch tryna steal our house!" the youngest Fontenot sister protested as she tried to get at her.

"This ain't our house! That's what I'm tryna tell you!" Buella said as she struggled to prevent a charge for assault.

"Huh?" the girl asked and frowned as the agent posted the sign.

"Yo granny left the house to Beatrice. And looks like she finna sell it?" Buella answered to her sister and asked towards the woman.

"I just got the listing an hour ago," she shrugged.

"That bitch must have called from the parking lot!" Buella said, shaking her head. In fact Beatrice called from the elevator before she even reached the lobby.

"Fuck this house!" Lil Baby decided and spun on her heels. She led the charge back into the house and plopped down in Big Mama's chair. It was the iron throne from which she ran the Crescent city with an iron fist.

"All the more reason to come to Atlanta!" Buella sighed and looked around the house. For all its splendor and amenities it was a dump as far as she was concerned.

"I'm just finna buy my own spot with the money granny left me," Lil Baby announced defiantly. Her chin was too high to notice the look on Buella's face when she made the announcement.

"What?" Alexis asked since she saw it.

"She ain't leave us no money," she replied.

"She what?" Lil Baby asked and almost fell out of the chair.

"Not a dime for me or her," Buella said, nodding towards Alexis. "You, she paid for college and said to holla at Mr Clyde when you finish."

"She 'musta set up a trust fund for you. All you gotta do is go to college!" Alexis replied enthusiastically. It actually sounded like a good idea, except for one thing.

"I ain't finna go to no college!" Lil Baby protested hotly.

"Chile, are you dumb or is you stupid!" Buella shot back. She left off the question mark since it wasn't a question. The girl was one or the other if she turned down a free ride through college. Most kids would love it but the trust fund attached to graduation made it even better.

"For real, cuz as smart as you are you can be done in three years!" Alexis added.

"Less if she go as hard in school as she did on the bull shit! And you can come to Atlanta to go to school," Buella sighed in frustration.

"I got business here. I'm ain't going nowhere!" Lil Baby proclaimed. She crossed her arms over her chest and turned her head like Big Mama used to do when she said what she said and that was the end of it.

A cold shiver shot up Buella's spine when she saw the look in her sister's eyes. She knew then she was too far gone to reach. Not without risking her own soul. That was more than she could afford to pay so she had to concede.

"Here..." Buella said as she dug into her purse. Lil Baby missed the defeat in her voice but it broke Alexis's heart.

"What's this?" Lil Baby asked before extending her hand to accept it.

"Yo ticket to Atlanta. Ain't got no date on it so just show up to the airport. Lil Baby was too proud to reach for it since accepting it meant accepting defeat. She was too proud and pride kills. Pride comes before the fall that her sister was trying to save her from. "Granny said it's only two ways out the streets, here's a third...."

The room went silent as she placed the ticket on the table next to the chair. Right on top of the pistol on the table. Lil Baby turned her head so she wouldn't have to watch her sister walk out of her life once again. Once again she caught an attitude about her sister leaving her in times of need.

"Bitch just selfish!" Lil Baby snarled. She sounded just like their grandmother who said the exact same thing from this exact same chair.

"Which one?" Alexis asked since there was more than one selfish Fontenot sister in the city.

～

"**W**hat the fuck now..." Lil Baby sighed in exasperation when she heard vehicles pulling into the driveway. Her first instinct was to grab the chopper and go to war but luckily Alexis looked out the window.

"Put that down!" she warned and looked around for anything that could get them in trouble.

"Who is it?" Lil Baby asked and put the Draco back down.

"Sheriff department!" the voice boomed over the loud knock.

"Sheriff?" Lil Baby wondered as she stomped over and snatched the door open. "What the hell you want?"

"Want? What I want wouldn't matter cuz this paper says I got to clear this house," he replied and extended the eviction notice.

"Ion want that!" Lil Baby fussed as if fussing could stop what was happening here. It wouldn't and he would remove her by force if he had to.

"Let me see this?" Alexis demanded and took the notice. Her eyes blinked as she read the legal documents that would empty the house. The truck with moving men was behind him in the driveway. "Well y'all cain't take her shit!"

"Whatever you want to take you need to take now. I need to clear this property and put the padlock on it," he announced and looked at his watch. "And I mean now."

"We gotta go Agatha. Grab your stuff!" Alexis explained and rushed to the back. She had amassed quite a bit of things in the weeks she had been staying and quickly grabbed a load. Lil Baby was stuck in place as she now read the documents.

"Auntie put the folks on us!" she reeled once she finally understood.

"Yes, and we gotta go!" Alexis replied as she carried her second load to her car.

"Let em get the..." Lil Baby began but looked over to the empty security house. Ethyl pulled the men since she didn't intend on paying them to guard the house anymore. She realized she was on her own and rushed to gather her own belongings. She had way more than would fit in her car but she did have cash.

"Yes?" the officer asked skeptically as the young woman approached.

"How much does it cost to buy me an extra couple of days?" she asked and produced a wad of cash. She had seen her granny change rules and policies in the same way many times.

"A couple hundred can get you a couple hours. Not days," he replied and licked his thin lips. The best he could do was move her to the back of his daily list which would give her until late afternoon.

"Two is a couple," Lil Baby sighed and peeled off two hundred dollars.

"Load up fellas. We'll come back to this one after Mulberry lane," the sheriff told his men. They were paid by the hour so it didn't matter how those hours were spent.

"Where are you going!" Alexis called after her sister when she jumped into her car and pulled away. She just shook her head and continued loading her car.

"This bitch..." Lil Baby grumbled and growled all the way over to the hotel her aunt was staying in during her stay in the city. She had hoped to have collected her money by now and be back out west. But no, now she had to fight. And fight she would until she had everything she felt was hers.

"How can I help you?" the clerk asked the angry young woman marching into the swank hotel. Security was poised to drag her out if the smiles didn't work.

"I'm here to see my auntie!" Lil Baby demanded. It dawned on her that the smiling woman wouldn't know which one of their guests was her auntie so she expounded, "Beatrice Fontenot!"

"Is she expecting you?" the clerk asked while pulling up the name. Lil Baby didn't answer so she made the call.

"Send her up," Beatrice announced when she answered. She was indeed expecting at least a call from her niece but wasn't surprised by her pulling up in person. In retrospect she wouldn't expect anything less. A few minutes later she heard the knock on the door and went to pull it open. "Hey dere."

"Hey dere hell! What you got going on auntie? How is the police at my house telling me I gotta go!" Lil Baby demanded.

"First things first. My house. I been paid for that house!" Beatrice replied. She paid with her hymen and dignity time and time again from the abuse she suffered in that house.

"Even if, you know I stay there. Been staying there. Where am I supposed to go?" she shot back.

"See, you are so used to folks taking care of you, you forget there comes a time when you gots to take care of yo self. It's that time now," Beatrice taught and paused for a moment for that to sink in. A slight nod told her the girl was following so she led some more. "As for where to go, college. Get whatever that woman left for you and be happy!"

"I ain't going to no college! I put in work 'round this city! I'm finna run this city!" she vowed as she had been since she got under her grandmother's wing.

"Sit down lil gurl!" Beatrice snapped. She stepped forward and got in her face so she only had two choices. She could either fight or sit down. She chose the latter and sank to the sofa with a sigh. "Look, niece..."

Beatrice paused and searched for the right words to sum up her nearly forty years on the planet. She had been raped, prostituted herself, sold herself and given herself away. She experimented with weed which led her to alcohol until she tried a line of coke. Then a hit of crack, a dab of smack until she was shooting Speedballs in between shooting porn scenes.

Her mouth opened, then closed a second later to swap out some words for some other words. The truth is the streets would eat this girl alive. Coming up under Big Mama exposed her to infamy but still didn't prepare her for that life. Her grandmother knew it too, which is why she set her up for college. She hoped the streets would turn her off but only turned her out.

"You not 'bout that life chile," Beatrice sighed. "You survived this long only cuz God protects babies and fools. You both, but you are not a baby no 'mo! These niggas will put you in a box 'fo they take orders from you!" she explained.

"How you know I ain't put no niggas in no box myself?" Lil Baby dared and cocked her head. Beatrice nodded in agreement that she probably had. It nodded some more since she knew her mother would have held her hand while she pulled the trigger. Just like she had done when she fired the bullet into Clarence's head.

"Well, like I said, you are not a baby no more. Do what you do. That's what I'm fixing to do. I'ma sell that haunted house from hell. Then I'ma get this money Miss Ethyl stole from my mama..." she stated plainly.

"What money?" Lil Baby perked up. "Cuz if she stole from her she stole from me too!"

"Well, help me get it and I'll share it," Beatrice offered since it might save her some time. Getting back to LA was worth ten percent in her opinion

"I'll help you find it and you split it with me!" she corrected. The slight tilt of her head suggested she knew something Beatrice didn't .

"Half then," Beatrice shot back quickly and extended her hand.

"Half," Lil Baby smiled and nodded. She stood and exited the room to head back over to the house. The moving men hadn't returned yet so they managed to load all of their clothing and etceteras into their vehicles. They shuttled back and forth to Alexis's grandmother's but Lil Baby had no intention on staying there.

CHAPTER SIX

"**C**an I help you young lady?" a well dressed man asked when Lil Baby entered the leasing office. Mr Shein

"Yes sir. I want to rent an apartment," she replied and smiled.

"How old are you?" he wondered since he would have guessed sixteen. Despite the professional attire and cleavage she still had the face of a child.

"However old I need to be..." she replied and placed a brown paper sack on the desk. His head tilted curiously before the words reached his mouth.

"What is this?" he asked and scrunched his face in genuine confusion. Now it was her turn to be confused since she knew he was in her grandmother's network.

"I'm kin to Big Mama..." she verbally slid across the table but dropping the name didn't unscrunch his face. "Eleanor, Fontenot?"

"But, she's deceased," he explained, which explained that their relationship was just as dead. Lil Baby assumed as much which was why she bought the paper sack stuffed with cash.

"Yeah, so are the men in these pictures..." she alluded to the dead presidents. "Ten thousand times over."

"Hmp," the man huffed since ten thousand dollars spoke louder than dropping a dead woman's name. "That could handle the application process..."

"But?" she asked in the pause he left for her to ask.

"But one bedroom units here cost twenty five hundred a month," he began in a tone that said that wasn't all to be said. Once again he left a pause for her to overcome that burden before moving on to another obstacle to hurdle.

"No problem," she quickly shot back. She had plenty of money put up as well as plenty more that should be coming in. "And what else?"

"You're definitely kin to Miss Fontenot!" he laughed when the bright girl picked up on his inflection. His eyes fluttered as he searched for a delicate way of putting forth his next request. "Your grandmother and I had, uh, a um, an arrangement, an understanding..."

"Ewwww!" Lil Baby grimaced before she could catch herself. Yet another example of just how not ready she was for what she was after. After all she had been naive enough to think the Family would line up and bend the knee as their new queen. When in fact they had broken into factions and fractions, each getting what they could get.

"Oh no! Not a um, physical understanding. I mean it was but not um, not she and I. She would provide um, company for me?" he asked and wiggled his brows.

"Girls? Ok, I can do that!" she cheered. A smile began to spread on her face until she registered that there was still more to come.'"What?"

"I like them um, young," he whispered sheepishly.

"How young?" Lil Baby asked as she cocked her head and squinted her eyes.

"Not kids!" he assured and raised his hands in surrender. "I mean pubescent, just young."

"Nigga you..." she began but caught herself. She needed him so she would give him what he wanted. Even if she didn't know how she would do it. She was finding out her late grandmother had no morals. There was a line drawn and she would have to cross it to follow in her footsteps. "Nigga I got you! Whatever you want!"

"In that case, let me show you to your unit..." Mr Shein cheered and hopped to his feet. Lil Baby was busy racking her brain about how to supply his request. She hadn't pimped her friends in a while and had no idea where to get one. Especially a young one. She was ready to quit and find another spot until Mr Shein opened the door. "And here we are..."

"Whoa!" Lil Baby gushed and ran over to the floor to ceiling windows. The unit had a spectacular view of the winding Mississippi river below. Even better was a good view of the condo building where Ethyl purchased with the money she skimmed over the years. The money she planned to split with her aunt once they found it.

"Hopefully I can 'Whoa' as well?" the man asked and rubbed his small, wrinkled hands together like a greedy housefly.

"Yeah, I um, I'm on it..." she replied. They handled the paperwork that got Lil Baby her first apartment.

~

"**H**ey dere?" Micah asked curiously when he answered the knock
at the door. He hadn't seen this particular face in a particularly
long time and wondered about the timing.

"Hey Micah. Is Miss Katie in?" Lil Baby asked. She sounded tenta-
tive and didn't like it one bit. She remembered she was a boss now and
puffed her chest out as she walked in.

"Lil Baby?" Katie asked and seemed just as surprised to see her.

"Been a minute since I made collections, but since Big Mama
gone..." Lil Baby sighed and summed up why she was here. She saw the
tacit conversation between the two in their glances. Then turned to
Katie to get it directly. "Something wrong?"

"Wrong? Naw, just different," she decided. Micah nodded like he
liked the sound of it so she continued. "Since Big Mama is not with us
anymore, God bless the dead. We are going off on our own now."

"Like Sugar Bear did that time?" Lil Baby asked curiously. She added
an air of naïveté on top like sprinkles on an ice cream cone, but didn't
make the veiled threat any more palatable.

"Naw we not going out bad like Sugar Bear!" Micah boomed and
moved forward like he might move on the girl.

"I'm sure we can figure something out?" Katie offered and waved
her security guard off.

"That's what I was hoping for," Lil Baby replied, since it was better
than pulling the gun from her purse. She knew she couldn't get where
she was trying to go without putting a few people in boxes and bags but
was open to negotiation. Even she knew her grandmother pushed too
hard and took too much. Which was why more of the people at her
funeral were happy to see her go.

"Yo granny took half. You cain't have that much!" Katie barked and
tilted her head in defiance.

"And I wouldn't want half!" she assured. "I'm thinking more like a
barter?"

"Dope for skin?" Micah asked enthusiastically.

"Services for services. I like that!" Lil Baby cheered as if it was his
idea even though it was exactly what she had in mind.

"So, no points? No percentage?" Katie dared.

"Nope. Just send a gal over to Mr Shein..." Lil Baby said and gave
the address.

"He likes em young," Katie nodded knowingly since she had been
supplying pubescent skin to him for years.

"Don't they all," Micah sighed and shook his head.

"They do?" the girl asked but this time the naïveté was real. She still didn't understand why older men had a penchant for younger girls. She listened intently as he ranted about R Kelly, Russell Simmons and Ditty but all she heard was dollars and cents.

"You be safe nah..." Katie called after Lil Baby as she left the house. She felt good about the arrangement since not being affiliated put her at risk from one of the other crime families. A power play was happening all across the city and she didn't want to get caught in the middle of it.

"It's not me you need to worry about," Lil Baby huffed and headed to her car.

She was out of the loop as of late so she didn't know where any of the many trap houses were located. Her grandmother let her run her own little schemes and scams so she would stay out of her business. She did know who would know and knew where he lived. Big Mama made it a point to know where everyone actually lived opposed to where they stayed. She had an address book of real addresses where her people really laid their heads. Lil Baby now had it and wasn't afraid to pull up.

～

"Someone pulling up," Little Tony reported to his father.

"Here?" Tony asked since he never had company at his real house. He kept a modest house in the city for business but this one out in Gretna was personal. It was where he lay his head with his wife and kid.

"What's wrong?" his wife reeled when he tucked a pistol into his waist and headed for the door.

"Nothing! Just stay inside," he barked and headed to confront the threat head on. There was a power struggle going on and he wanted to make sure it didn't reach his porch. The gun was tucked but wouldn't be needed when he saw who was pulling up. "What are you doing here?"

"Here to talk to you since you ain't been by to talk to me," Lil Baby replied. There was a moment of silence while he answered the unasked question of how she knew where he lived. Big Mama made it her business to know where her people laid their heads. Just in case she had to have them and their family killed if they violated her Family.

The trap houses were disposable and changed weekly and sometimes daily. But the stash spots and cook houses remained the same. As did the list of houses of employees.

"Yeah I um, been dealing with Ethyl on everything," he said, hoping

34

to shift the blame to her since they had been splitting the drug proceeds fifty/fifty.

"I ain't seen my granny share since we buried her?" Lil Baby asked but it wasn't really a question. "I reckon I'll get mine soon. In the meanwhile I need some product."

"You? I thought you didn't..." Tony began but remembered they were on his front porch. Obviously she could do whatever she wanted to do if she came here. He could either kill her or play her game, for now. "I'll send Rage to..."

"Um..." Lil Baby hummed. She was learning as she went along and realized she needed another spot for business. She pulled her new phone and pulled up the new number to her new phone to pass along. "Have him call me..."

Tony stood there long after Lil Baby got back into her car and pulled away. He let out a deep sigh as he looked around his quiet neighborhood. It was nothing like the inner city blocks he helped destroy with the crack and smack he pushed to pay for the nice house. He let out another sigh at the thought of having to move.

"Shole would be a lot easier to just send you with yo granny..." he allowed in the direction she just left. That was a call he couldn't make so he pulled his phone and made another call.

"Hey," the recipient answered when she took the call.

"Guess who just came to see me? At my house," Tony asked.

"Agatha," Ethyl replied and shook her head. She had hoped the girl would go with her sister but no such luck.

"Yes. To my house!" he reeled.

"Guess she'll be to see me next," Ethyl sighed.

"She wants some product, and Big Mama share. What you want me to do?" he asked since she called shots for now.

"Give her what she wants," she sighed and clicked off. She was right about one thing since she was about to have company herself.

CHAPTER SEVEN

'Mmhm' Lil Baby hummed smugly as she pulled up to Ethyl's new digs. She was feeling quite proud of herself for pulling up on people like this while she had the advantage of no one knowing where she lay her head these days.

She was feeling herself so hard she didn't notice the gun pointed at the back of her head when she stepped out of her car. The finger on the trigger slowly squeezed until there was just a whisper between her and that plot next to her grandmother. Ethyl could end her there but wouldn't. Instead she tucked the pistol and called her name.

"Hey dere Agatha," It was all she could do not to laugh at the surprise on the girl's face when she saw she wasn't quite as smart as she thought. Actually, she was plenty smart. Just predictable is all. Especially to people who had been in these streets for decades.

"Hey," Lil Baby replied with a sliver of a quiver in her timbre. She heard the fear and cleared her throat to remove it before continuing. "Can I have a word with you?"

"Fuck naw!" Ethyl growled and quickly closed the distance between them. She was a few inches taller than the teen so she leaned in close enough to smell the garlic from the chicken fricassee she had for lunch. It mixed with the malice and made the girl wince as did the harsh words to come. "Fuck naw you cain't have no word! Pulling up to folks' houses like you intimidating folks? Like yo granny taught you! But who do you think taught yo granny?"

"It doesn't matter who taught me, as long as I know!" Lil Baby shot back as defiantly as she could but the fear still rang loud and clear like the church bells in the distance.

"You don't know shit! You stupid lil bitch! So smart til you stupid! Take yo ass to school! Or go to Atlanta with Buella! Shit, go to Atlanta and go to school!" Ethyl growled but the stubborn girl was undeterred.

"I want what's mine! My granny schooled me to take her place! I..." she was saying until the woman reeled back and slapped the words down her throat.

"You stupid lil bitch yo granny schooled you so you would stay out the streets! She let you have yo lil fun but you tryna end up like yo sisters? That smack damn near kilt yo sister! Bella got herself killed playing with these street niggas and they tender ass feelings! That's all that's out here. Death! Death and jail!" the woman sighed.

"And I ain't scared of either!" Lil Baby replied and tilted her head to show the woman she actually wasn't as smart as she thought she was.

"There's worse than that chile. You tryna end up in hell with the rest of us," she sighed and shook her head. "That's where yo granny is. Hell. Yo daddy, hoe ass mama. All in hell."

"I want what's mine or we'll all go to hell together!" Lil Baby proclaimed. Ethyl turned and looked at the entrance to her building and sighed again. The cameras would clearly catch her putting a bullet in her head so it would have to wait.

"Here chile..." she said as she dug into her purse. Lil Baby didn't flinch since she didn't think the woman would harm her.

"What's that?" she asked of the large roll of cash.

"Yo allowance," she replied and extended the cash. Lil Baby wouldn't reach for it so she shoved it down her shirt. "Yo granny gave you a thousand a week. I'm giving you two. Now, you stay from here. Don't come back to my house again or fuck them cameras!"

"Oh yeah! Well I..." Lil Baby fussed as she walked away. Along with her went any chance of recovering the money she skimmed over the years.

~

"Hmp. Sho nuff. Gurl..." Beatrice interjected from time to time as Lil Baby filled her in.

"And they cut me out of the business. Got me on allowance like I'm a dang baby!" she pouted.

"Cuz you is," her aunt replied and kept it a buck. "I ain't finna let her take from my mama..."

Lil Baby watched the woman's face contort as she plotted. She had made several hundred thousand off the sale of the house but this wasn't about money. "It's the principle!"

"Hmp!" Lil Baby huffed. She spent enough time in the mirror to know greed when she saw it. As well as the new look looking back at her lately. The look of vengeance that can only be slacked by revenge. She dreamt of killing Rue each night but only heard reports of sightings each day. She heard he was hanging out at a local club lately and decided she would soon go clubbing herself.

"Well, you did what you could do," Beatrice sighed. It sounded like defeat but was anything but. She had been doing her homework too and had a plan of her own. "Guess I'll be heading back to Cali. What you finna do gurl?"

"Get what I got coming," she shot back as defiantly as ever.

"Yeah, thing about that tho..." Beatrice began but changed her mind. She knew you got what you give and if the girl kept putting negativity into the universe negativity was all she had coming back. "Mama used to say you can't tell if you got enough salt by looking. You gotta taste it."

"Yeah, but what does that mean?" Lil Baby wondered. She had heard Big Mama tell her that on many occasions but never understood. "Ion get it?"

"You will," Beatrice said and stood. She hugged her niece tightly and hoped it wouldn't be the last time. The girl was destined to get a taste of what she was putting out and she just hoped it didn't kill her.

Her shoulders shrugged once she was alone but she didn't abandon her booth. She had invited the last of the Hot-gurls to join her so it wasn't long until Choo-choo walked in. She had a slight limp in her gait as she came over.

"Hey gurl!" Choo-choo cheered and hugged her neck.

"Hey yo self!" Lil Baby squealed and returned the hug. "What's wrong with your leg?"

"Nothing. My big dick boyfriend got me sore," she cackled. Lil Baby joined her which made it even more funny since she was talking about her ex. Rue had just beat her back out before hitting the streets to make his rounds.

"Hmp!" Lil Baby replied and recalled being sore after sex herself not long ago. She had a date with that same dingaling the night he murdered her grandmother instead.

Choo-choo was falling in love with more than just the dingaling tho. Rue didn't just lay some A-1 pipe; he kept her pocket, purse and closets filled. She was now wearing the same labels as her on time boss. Rue on the other hand was incapable of love. He wanted to love Lil Baby and felt a flutter in his heart when he saw her. But it was overruled by the murderous revenge bubbling through his soul.

Choo-choo was a means to an end since she kept him informed of Lil Baby's whereabouts. He wouldn't lift a finger to harm her but needed to make sure she didn't do anything to harm him either. The fact that the sex was good didn't hurt anything either.

"You good gurl?" Choo-choo asked and pulled her back into the present.

"Who? Huh? Hell yeah!" she proclaimed once she got her thoughts together. She was everything but ok but wasn't going to let her know that.

"You need to hit the club with me!" Choo-choo cheered and danced in her seat at the notion. Just the thought of shaking her ass made her shake her ass in her chair.

"Ok," Lil Baby replied quickly. So quickly her so-called friend missed it.

"You don't know what you be missing! All the players be up in there!" she vowed. She kept hoping that she would find someone else so she could have Rue to herself. She knew the girl lived rent in his head but nothing lived in his black heart. "That nigga Baws pulled up in a dang G-wagon! White on white with white rims, seats..."

'Hmp?' Lil Baby thought to herself. She knew the name Baws well since Rue loathed the dude. They did time in juvenile detention and bumped heads. Baws won the fist fight but Rue won the war when he got put on with the Family. Baws was forced to take his hustle out of the city but that seemed to be working out just fine. The same crack and smack sold for double and triple out in the burbs and parishes. The Family had the city but Baws was sowing up the rest of the state.

"He was iced out too! His neck, wrist..." Choo-choo went on. She left out the part about Baws winking at her to mock Rue. Rue saw it but didn't care enough about Choo-choo to care. They would eventually bump heads, it just wouldn't be over Choo-choo.

"I said I'm coming, gurl!" Lil Baby forced her way back into the conversation.

"You for real!" Choo-choo gushed. "Shoot, I should come to yo house and spin a night!"

"Gurl, I ain't finna have no sleep over! We not twelve no more!" Lil Baby laughed the idea off. The fact is she knew her life depended upon people not knowing where she lay her head. Which was exactly why Rue kept pushing her to find that out. "I'll see you at the club."

CHAPTER EIGHT

"Looks like someone still got it..." Ethyl nodded at her reflection as she inspected herself for the night. She had squeezed into a tight dress that pushed mounds of good titty meat out the top. Then turned to the side to check out the booty. It was right so she gave it a slap. "Ass nice and fat!"

Ethyl convinced herself she deserved a night out. Beatrice called to say goodbye before boarding her flight back to LA and Lil Baby had been placated with an allowance. Not having to kill people she had loved was definitely a reason to celebrate.

"Shoooot..." Ethyl huffed at the thought of getting laid too. It had been a while since she had a certified plumber lay some good pipe.

Big Mama kept a boy toy around for that reason but had the worst luck in picking them. She had a bad track record of picking men who would fuck her but also fuck over her kids, finances or business. Several of them ended up in the swamp but it was Ethyl who learned a lesson from it.

Her vagina throbbed to give its vote and the matter was settled. She reached down and slid her panties back off since they would be coming off by the end of the night anyway. Her brow furrowed as she ran through the 'who can I fuck' rolodex in her head. She shook her head at the aging list of aging men. Most were married, dead or still in jail so they wouldn't do at all.

"Hmp," she huffed and lifted her chin when she decoded on some young man with some young meat. She didn't know who yet but set out to go find him.

Young meat wouldn't be hard to find since she was pushing the expensive whip and dipped in diamonds and old school gold. The valet stepped forward to open her door and park her car when she arrived at the club.

"Here you go..." Ethyl sang as she stepped wide legged from her vehicle. She gave a clear view of her old lady box but the young attendant didn't take her up on it. He liked vaginas just fine, just liked them younger.

"Thank you ma'am," he said as he traded places with her and pulled away to park.

"Faggot..." she muttered from him not taking her up on the offer.

"Is that Miss Ethyl!" the burly bouncer exclaimed when he saw her approach. He quickly removed the velvet rope to grant her access.

"Thank you Robert," she smiled and sized him up. She recalled a romp she had three decades ago with a bodybuilder type like him. He was all upper torso, pecs and abs but lacking below the belt. She shook the thought off and stepped inside.

"Miss Ethyl! Is everything ok?" the owner asked as he rushed to her side.

"Shole is. Just came for a night out," she explained. He had some explaining of his own and quickly copped a plea.

"I wasn't sure who to give that to now that Big Mama is, you know..." he offered. Ethyl furrowed her brow and caught on. Big Mama had a piece of this club without her knowledge.

"Hmp!" she huffed at the notion of the woman being mad at her for skimming when she was skimming herself. Never mind that it was Big Mama's business, they were still supposed to be partners. "Don't worry about it for now."

"Right this way!" he cheered and led her to his VIP section. He shooed a couple out of the best booth and put her in it instead. He raised a hand and the pretty waitress abandoned another table and rushed over. "Your money's no good here. Get her whatever she wants!"

"I'll have a bottle of Dom," she ordered and leaned back. Ever the business woman she scanned the area and took a quick count of how much money they were making. The waitresses and bartenders were hopping to fill glasses and orders. The kitchen was turning out seafood platters every few minutes as well.

"Finna get me a piece of this..." she decided when the waitress returned. "Thank you sweetie."

"Thank you!" the girl gushed and clutched the hundred dollar tip. "If you need anything else, just let me know!"

"I'm sure this will do for me," she assured since she was never much of a drinker. The girl turned to leave but Ethyl spotted something else she wanted. Needed even since the tall, dark and handsome man was staring right at her. "Bring me that chunk of chocolate right there."

"Damn! I know that's right!" the girl laughed when she saw the handsome stranger. This was an older spot but it wasn't unusual for younger people to hang out. Of both sexes since the older patrons bought as much dick as pussy. It was known for sugar daddies as well as sugar mamas.

Ethyl sat back smugly and basked in the accolades from the people coming to pay homage. She was drunk off power before the waitress returned with her bottle as well as that chunk of chocolate she ordered.

"Here you are ma'am..." the waitress sang as she popped the cork and poured two flutes. The handsome young man stood by looking pretty.

"Thank you chile," Ethyl thanked with a hundred dollar bill. She was showing off a little for her guest but it felt like it ain't tricking when you got it. "Have a seat handsome..."

"Thank you," he smiled whitely in contrast to his black skin.

"What's yo name boy?" she demanded so he understood she was the type who made demands. She had some demands in mind already. Like deeper, harder, and lick it, once she got him home.

"Whatever you want it to be," he replied with a sassy smile that made her wonder if he went both ways. Her throbbing box had already chosen so she pressed on.

"I'll call you, Chuck," she decided, then explained. "Chuck and I hope you can fuck!"

"Believe it or not, I came here tonight just to fuck you," he offered along with that smile again. Old Ethyl's lonely box started beating like a drum and she had heard enough. She tossed back the flute of bubbly and stood.

"Let's get out of here!" she demanded.

"Let's," Chuck agreed and stood. Tony was already standing by, talking to the same pretty waitress about some fucking as well. Ethyl didn't trust her security to anyone but him after she saved his life from Big Mama.

"I'm ok," Ethyl assured and waved him off when he started to follow them from the club. He locked eyes with the stranger and debated the order.

"Where are you going?" the waitress pouted when he took off after the new boss.

"Keep it hot for me lil bit..." he said over his shoulder as he headed out. Ethyl's car had just pulled off when he hit the sidewalk. He sent for his car anyway and took off in the same direction.

"You live near here?" Ethyl asked from the passenger seat of her own car. She was stupid horny but not stupid enough to take the stranger to her own spot.

"Not really," he said and reached over to entertain her for the ride.

"Oh!" Ethyl reeled when he reached under her dress. She spread her legs wide to grant access to the juice box bubbling below. Ethyl bust a long overdue nut before they reached the next red light. She would bust two more before they reached the secluded house out in the country.

"Here we are," he announced and came around to open her door.

"You live on a dang farm?" she fussed and scrunched her nose at the sounds and smells of farm animals.

"No," he replied despite leading her towards the well appointed farm house. It was pitch black when he opened the door and stepped aside so she could enter.

"Surprise!" the room erupted when the lights suddenly came on. Ethyl almost smiled at the surprise party until she registered the faces. There wasn't a wisp of mirth on any of the faces in the room.

"The fuck y'all got going on!" Ethyl demanded, still in boss mode. She tried to back out of the house but Chuck blocked the way.

"You know I couldn't go home without saying bye!" Beatrice sang with a smile on her face that contradicted the gun in her hand.

"I just came to watch," Lil Baby shrugged. "This is her duck, I'm finna watch her pluck."

"That ain't even how yo granny used to say it!" Ethyl shot back as if mauling the woman's statement mattered. It didn't.

"You can still get through this, you know?" Beatrice offered softly. After all, she had known the woman all of her life. "Just come off that money."

"You're still gonna kill me if I do!" Ethyl shot back knowingly since she knew she would. "Let me go and I'll take you to it."

"You'll take us to the money?" Lil Baby asked with wide eyed naivety. Then looked at her auntie and they cracked up. "Not!"

"Well do what you do then!" Ethyl declared and put up her dukes. She would fight them both thirty rounds but Chuck sucker punched her from behind and turned out her lights.

"Thank you Darius," Beatrice sang. "If you can take her out to the pen we'll take it from here."

"Yes'm ma'am," he replied and hoisted the sleeping woman onto his shoulder. He was paid well enough to disregard his fancy shoes and get down and dirty. He did what he did and looked toward Beatrice for his next order.

"We'll take it from her," she smiled and winked and sent him on his way. She had a few minutes so she kicked it with her niece. "I like yo outfit!"

"Thank you!" Lil Baby cheesed and did a spin in her tight leather shorts and designer T-shirt. It was a little mature for the club she was heading to but so was she. They made the most of their time together until Ethyl awoke.

"Un-uh!" the prissy woman grunted when she awoke. It was the smell that snapped her from her slumber before the pain of being socked registered. "Owe!"

"I bet! Ole Darius shole do pack a punch," Beatrice chuckled. "I hate you ain't get the dick first, but I got a flight to catch."

"And I'm going to the club!" Lil Baby cheered with enthusiasm.. She was giddy about going out even if she had business on her mind.

"What y'all gals got going on? Don't do it like this!" Ethyl moaned when she recognized the stench and sounds of her surroundings. She was seated against a post with her hands tied, in the middle of a pig pen.

The mud and pig shit ruined her dress but the hungry hogs in the pen were a bigger problem. They could eat a body to nothing in a matter of minutes. "This ain't right!"

"Says the woman who fed my friend to Bella," Lil Baby protested. She had no idea she killed Jernika until Patty-cake tried to kill her for it. And died along with her baby right in front of her eyes.

"Last chance..." Beatrice threatened and held up the box with the button that would release the hungry hogs.

"Fuck you!" Ethyl shot back. There was no way she would let her live even if she did come off the cash. She lifted her chin defiantly and Beatrice pressed the button.

"Dang!" Lil Baby reeled when the pigs rushed out and attacked.

"They don't call them hogs for nothing!" Beatrice remarked and the animals dismembered and disfigured the woman right before their eyes. Even the little piggies snapped off fingers and toes to get a taste. There would be nothing left in a few minutes but neither had time to wait.

"I got a flight to catch," Beatrice repeated over the grunts and squeals.

"Call me when you get home nah," her niece insisted. "I'm finna go shake my ass!"

CHAPTER NINE

"Dang!" Lil Baby exclaimed and turned to the side. She remembered how Bella used to marvel at her own ass and now she was doing the same. It looked right in the tight, suede shorts with all that good yellow thigh exposed.

She glossed her thick lips to a sheen and flipped the one bouncy curl on the side of her head. Then stuck her chest out like she used to do when she first sprouted nubs. It wasn't needed anymore since she grew a set of plump breasts that stood out on their own.

"Hmp!" she huffed and remembered why she was going out in the first place. Rue would be there and she couldn't live until he was dead. There was no place to hide a gun in the tiny shorts or tight T-shirt so she tucked it into her purse and headed out.

Lil Baby looked over towards Ethyl's building and shook her head. Her shoulders shrugged on their own but they were right. This was on her for switching up and stealing from her granny. Her chin lifted and she continued on to her car. Her phone buzzed as she got in and she twisted her lips at the name on the screen. They were still twisted when she took the call.

"Hey gurl!" Lil Baby greeted.

"Where you at? I thought you was coming to the club!" Choo-choo pouted through the line. The music boomed in the background since she was already there.

"I said I might and I might," she shrugged even if the girl couldn't see it.

"Well you should cuz it's lit!" Choo-choo cheered and bounced her ample ass.

"I might..." Lil Baby replied and clicked off. She learned a long time ago never to give up too much information. The music in the background inspired her to turn the radio on and up and her own ass began to shake in her seat. She bent corners by memory since she needed no GPS to navigate her city. The city she was one step closer to claiming since Ethyl would be pig shit by the morning.

Her mind raced faster than the scenery out her window and she arrived without a plan. She had a gun and good looks and that was better than nothing. The club didn't have a valet but she got lucky when a spot opened up right across the street as she pulled up. Some guy had gotten lucky with some girl and rushed to get her home.

She pulled in but stopped to survey her surroundings before getting out. She plotted an escape route by car and on foot just in case she got lucky too and was able to put a bullet in Rue's head. A deep sigh escaped her chest when she saw the bouncers searching both the men and women. One had a police type metal detector wand which he waved over each patron. Including the women and their purses. That meant she wasn't getting in with the gun so she slid it under her seat and hopped out.

'Pssshhh!' Lil Baby hissed at the cat calls coming from the thugs in the line. She was used to them by now but never understood why men did it. Like, did calling out 'hey sexy' 'excuse miss lady' ever actually work for them. One thing she was sure of was she wasn't standing in that long ass line.

"Line down there..." a female bouncer grunted and nodded her big head down the block.

"Yeah, un-uh," Lil Baby corrected and passed her a hundred dollar bill.

"You good," the woman said and quickly tucked the bill before waving her inside.

"Shit!" Lil Baby fussed when the woman didn't even search her or her purse. Which means she could have gotten her gun inside. She almost wanted to go back and get it but shook the idea from her head. Only fools rushed in and she no fool. Foolish for sure, but there's a difference.

It was her foolishness that allowed her to let the killer get that close to her grandmother. She should have told Big Mama who he was the second she found out who Rue was related to. She would probably have killed him but that was ok. Now she had to do it herself. She still blamed Rue instead of herself. He was on her mind just as he invaded her vision. Rue was across the club groping some jet black chick and whispering nasty nothings in her ear.

'Grrrr...' Lil Baby growled as she looked around for weapons. She saw she could use it to bludgeon him but shook that idea from her head.

"Hey gurl!" Choo-choo cheered and hugged her neck from the side. She nearly got tackled for startling the girl.

"Hey..." Lil Baby replied but kept her eyes glued on her target.

"Don't worry about him! Too many rich niggas in here to be sweating no ex!" Choo-choo assured her. She and Rue had a fluidly open relationship since she was a hoe. In fact she planned to join him and the black chick when he took her home for a threesome.

"Ain't nobody sweating him!" she vowed and rolled her eyes. Lil Baby's eyes rolled around the club but got caught in the brilliant flash of diamonds coming from a brown skin dude. Several chicks hovered and danced nearby hoping for his attention but he was too busy returning text in between sips on his drink.

"That's Baws!" Choo-choo explained when she followed her eyes over to the man. "Rue cain't stand his ass!"

"He can't?" Lil Baby asked out her mouth while, 'how you know?' swirled in her head.

"Un-uh," Choo-choo grimaced and shook her head. That answered the external question but Lil Baby would reserve the tacit question for later. Until then she acted instinctively and walked away. She put a little extra sway in her hips which translated into a lot of wiggle in her ass.

"Yeah lil mama I'll fuck the..." Rue was saying when he looked up and saw Lil Baby headed his way. He instantly dropped his eyes to her hands since they contained a Draco machine gun the last time he saw her. They were empty this time and she walked right by without ever even looking his way.

"Get off ya phone!" Lil Baby demanded when she slid into the booth with Baws.

"Huh?" he winced and looked up from his transactions. He registered the cute chick then looked at his men and wondered how she was allowed to get so close. They were so busy soliciting some sex for the evening Lil Baby slipped right by them.

"I said get off yo phone!" she demanded and pulled it from his hand and placed it on the table. Baws furrowed his brow like he was searching for how he was supposed to feel. It took a few seconds for him to figure out she was flirting with him. Then another for him to place the face.

"I know who you are..." he nodded. He had a healthy respect for Big

Mama even though he never wanted to get down with the Family. He was his own boss and liked calling his own shots. Not to mention cute.

"Then shouldn't I know who you are?" she dared sassily.

"No!" he shot back and wiped the smile from her face. "What do you want?"

"I uh..." Lil Baby stammered and got stuck since she didn't expect that response.

"Un-huh. I heard y'all scrambling to control the city. Tryna recruit players on ya team?" he challenged.

"Nigga I'm out here to shake my ass!" Lil Baby shot back as she regained her composure. "I thought you were my type since you shining and shit but now I see why ain't nothing but niggas 'round you. If you gay just say that!"

Baws just blinked through the tirade until she was finished. People didn't usually speak to him like that since he was known to drop bodies for much less. A slow smile spread on his face as she stood to walk off. With plan A dead she already started plotting on plan B.

"Hole up lil mama," he decided and pulled her back by her hand.

"Hole up, what!" she demanded and snatched her hand away. Then contradicted the move by staying put.

"If you came to shake yo ass," he smiled and showed her what thirty grand can get in a grill. His diamond teeth glistened and he instructed, "Go and shake it..."

Lil Baby twisted her lips and almost walked away but the DJ just happened to throw on her favorite Mystical song. Plus Rue was locked on to her when she looked up. She began to pop, shimmy and shake, making his blood boil.

Rue didn't hear the black girl fuss him out before she walked off. It wasn't long until he had seen enough. Once Baws gave Lil Baby's ass a smack he stood to leave. They finally made eye contact as he left the club. The malice in his eyes cut through the dance floor as he headed out.

"Take my number..." Lil Baby demanded and picked his phone up. Baws's men looked curiously as she tapped her numbers into his phone and took off out the club. If she could catch up with Rue she could kill him herself. Either way the trap was set since she knew he would react about seeing her with his nemesis. Even if she kinda wanted to see Baws again herself.

"Shit!" she fussed when she rushed out and didn't see Rue. Only because he didn't want to be seen since he slinked down in the decked out Ram truck. He saw her though and pulled out after her.

Lil Baby took a guess and headed off in one direction. She realized she didn't even know what kind of car she was looking for but had the gun in her lap in case she found it. A few blocks later she turned in a different direction but came up with the same results. She wasn't sure if the truck behind her was following her or not so she blew through a red light to see if it would follow.

"Fuck!" Rue fussed when a cop car pulled behind her and lit up. He certainly couldn't afford to get stopped himself since he too had a gun on his lap.

"Shit!" Lil Baby repeated as she pulled over. She kept an eye on the truck as it turned off and went in another direction. She was so busy watching it she didn't notice the cop until he was standing beside her window.

"Do you know why I pulled you over?" the cop asked like cops ask. Then noticed the gun and put his hand on his own. "Why do you have a gun ma'am?"

"Do you know where we are?" Lil Baby asked and tilted her head curiously as if it were a stupid question.

"Yes?" he replied just as curiously.

"So why would you ask me why I have a gun? You have a gun..." she reminded. He didn't have an answer so he asked another question.

"Did you happen to see that red light you ran?" he asked.

"Yup. Saw that same truck following me for several blocks too," she said and looked over to where Rue had pulled over. She couldn't see who was behind the tinted glass but didn't need to see him to feel him.

"Shit!" Rue grumbled when the cop turned and looked as well. He pulled out and bent a corner. The cop decided he might be more interesting than blowing a red light so he hopped back into his car and pursued it.

"Sucka!" Lil Baby chuckled and went home for the night.

CHAPTER TEN

"Shit," Rue grumbled when he heard the loud knock on the door. He had taken shots at the cop who followed him last night and managed to get away. He disposed of the disposable vehicle and got another. He still clutched his gun as he approached the door. Probably an unnecessary precaution since only two people knew where he stayed. One was behind him in bed in a dick induced coma. The other was knocking on the door. "Sup woadie?"

"We got problems..." Tony sighed as he stepped in. He registered the gun in his hand but Rue tucked it away and they sat. The fact was they both knew they would either kill or be killed by the other one day. But in the interim they got money together.

"What's up?" Rue asked and braced himself for the bad news.

"It's Ethyl. She is not answering calls," he revealed.

"Ole ass prolly somewhere with some dick off in her!" Rue laughed hopefully.

"Yeah, nah tho," Tony replied with another sigh. He had hoped as much too until reports of her leaving the club with a man led to her disappearance. They had disappeared enough people to know they wouldn't be seeing her again. Not in this life anyway.

"So, shit..." Rue began and began to smile. "That's just one less cut to cut out. We can split this thang fiddy/fiddy!"

"Except," Tony said and sighed yet again. "Ion know who the connect is. Never met him. Only people ever got to go were Big Mama and Ethyl. Oh and..."

"Nuh-uh!" Rue reeled when he caught on. "Say it ain't so!"

"Shit, her granny took her along all the time," he recalled and nodded. The room went silent as they both thought of how they could get the information from Lil Baby. The same one they were just about to cut out altogether since Ethyl was out of the picture.

"Hmp, shit..." Rue huffed at his idea of just kidnapping the chick and beating it out of her.

"Nah, cuz we need her to make the buy. We cain't just roll up on them folk," Tony replied as if he read his mind. He didn't, they just thought alike. It was the opposite of great minds thinking alike because so do small minds.

"Yeah," Rue grunted as the rusty wheels in his head began to churn once more. One thing he was sure of was eventually robbing the connection once he found who it was. Just like he planned to kill Tony once he had the connect. His head shook when he realized what he needed to do.

"What?" Tony asked, hoping he had an answer.

"Guess we gotta cut the bitch back in. Start her off as a three way partner," he advised.

"Hmp?" Tony hummed and wondered at what point did they cut her off, and to what extent. This was a dirty game and no way to play it without getting dirt on you. "Guess I'll hit the girl up."

"I wouldn't let her know 'bout me," Rue advised since he was dumb enough to think Tony was dumb enough to do some dumb shit like that.

"Yeah, you're right..." he agreed, because he was. He stood and headed out the house to make the call. Rue got a bright idea and rushed back into the bedroom. He snatched the sheet from covering Choo-choo and admired her round ass. Hoe or no hoe the girl was fine. His dick jumped to life and he jumped onto her back.

"Huh?" Choo-choo wondered when he forced himself inside of her. Her body reacted quicker than her mind and got wet instantly. She arched her back and gave him full access inside of her.

"Shit!" Rue grunted and grinded. He thought of the time Lil Baby let him hit in this position and came instantly. "Shit!"

"Look like someone got some good pussy!" Choo-choo bragged and squeezed as he squirmed.

"Shole do!" he agreed. It was as close as he came to giving a compliment. He grinded some more and made his pitch. "I need you to link up with ole girl today. Tell me where y'all gone be."

"Ok babe," she replied instantly. She knew he still had feelings for Lil Baby but since they didn't stop him from breaking her off financially or dick wise. "I got you baby..."

~

"**E**thyl? No I ain't seen her! I ain't heard from her since last week," Lil Baby practiced as she drove downtown to the busy French Quarter to meet Tony. She didn't have any reason to distrust Tony which was just more proof that she wasn't ready for the life she was after. She still chose to meet in a crowded spot just like her granny taught her. Plus she had a lunch meeting after this meeting. "What do you mean missing? Oh my gawd!"

Lil Baby snickered in the mirror as she practiced being shocked and playing dumb. Even though she could still hear the crunch of cartilage and bone as the pigs made a meal of the woman. Justice since Ethyl shole loved her some pork. The skin, feet, ears and even intestines.

"From the rooter to the tooter!" she giggled at another of her grandmother's sayings and came to a stop. She scanned the area for danger before she put the car in park and stepped out. She was early as usual so she called her friend back to fill the time. Big Mama taught her never to kill time since time is your friend. It's more valuable than money.

"Hey gurl!" Choo-choo cheered when she took the call. "I'm getting dressed now."

"Ok. What y'all did after I left last night?" she asked even though she could care less. She did what she came to do and met Baws. Hopefully it made Rue mad enough to expose himself. She was ready to whack him whenever his head poked up like the whack-a-mole game in the arcade. Except she planned on using the hammer in her purse to put a bullet in her brain. She didn't hear much of whatever Choo-choo was Choo-choo-ing about but 'mmhm-ed' and 'Un-huh-ed' like she was fully invested.

"Mmhm, and them hoes was all over Baws!" she reported.

"He left with one of them?" she asked and heard the anguish in her own tone.

"Hell nah, he be chumping chicks off," Choo-choo shot back. She would know since she shot her shot at him too once Rue left the club. "Rue say he must like boys..."

"A'ight, I'll see you in a bit..." Lil Baby said when she spotted Tony pulling up. They were having lunch in the spot after this business meeting so she clicked off.

"Hey dere," Tony greeted solemnly when he arrived at the table. He pulled the empty seat and sat.

"What's wrong?" she asked and made the face she practiced on the way over. She knew it wasn't but asked anyway, "Is everything ok?"

"Naw, un-uh. I can't say that it is," he sighed and gave it to her straight. "Ethyl dead."

"Whaaaa! How? When? I mean, how?" Lil Baby asked and paid close attention to his response.

"Ion know none of that. Just know she's gone and she ain't finna just go, 'lest someone made her go," he said and she nodded.

"Think she will come back?" she asked even though she knew the answer to that one as well. The pig farm was just as efficient as the swamp. No one ever came back from either.

"Naw and that's what I need to talk to you about," he replied. She tilted her head curiously and he continued. "Ain't no one never been to the connect 'sides yo grammaw, Ethyl and you. 'Ifn we finna stay in business we need you to take me to make the buy."

'Well, well, well, would you look at this shit! These niggas wanted to cut me out but now they needs me!' Lil Baby thought to herself. The look on her face remained stoic while she danced and twerked in her mind. 'Shit, I'm finna tax the shit out these niggas! No, sell them the connect! Lease it for um, forty percent. No, fifty percent! Ain't no way in hell I'm finna take him to no connect tho...'

"Lil Baby?" Tony asked after several minutes of muted conversation inside her head.

"Huh? Oh nah I um. I need to think about that Tony. I mean, Ethyl didn't even pay me my allowance this week," she huffed.

"How much does she give you?" he asked and dug into his pocket.

"Ten thousand, a week," she shot back quickly.

"Shit, Ion got quite that much on me..." he said as he came out with the few grand he kept on him at all times. He thrust it forward in hopes it would suffice.

"Thanks but, this won't suffice," she replied and tucked the money into her purse and used the gun as a paperweight.

"I can brang you another ten in a few minutes. Just gotta run to the house and..." he was saying and standing.

"Naw, not just that," she froze him halfway seated and standing. "If you need me to make the buys, using my grammaw name, the money she left in the streets, her rep. I'ma need half. Half of everything that comes back!"

"Half!" Tony reeled and began shaking his head. "Can't do half. I can do, thirty percent. Same as yo granny took. The rest gotta spread around. So err body can eat."

"Spread the other fifty percent cuz it's half or nothing. Call me later and let me know," she directed and turned her face away just like Big Mama used to do when she said what she said and was done talking.

"Ok, yeah. I um, yeah," Tony stammered. He looked around the busy restaurant and realized how it would if he threw her over his shoulder and carried her away. "So call you later..."

Choo-choo entered the restaurant and passed by Tony in the door-way. He mumbled to himself and didn't notice her. He did notice Rue parked across the street and made a beeline over to him.

"Well?" Rue asked and cocked his head.

"Well nothing. Just chill and let me handle it!" he pleaded since Rue could make it worse. "You just get the bread together. We finna make a big buy!"

"Check," Rue nodded and started the car back up. He watched Tony walk away and turned the engine back off. His plan was still to follow Lil Baby and find out where she lay her head.

"Hey gurl!" Choo-choo sang and did a little twirl to show off her designer labels.

"Slay bih!" Lil Baby cheered but wasn't moved since she had worn the same outfit in high-school. She still had a lingering question in her head and contemplated on how best to ask without the girl knowing she asked.

"Lunch on me," Choo-choo insisted as directed. Rue explained how spoiled the girl was and that the best way to get something out of her was to get her what she wanted.

"Bet, cuz I'm hungry!" Lil Baby cheered and picked up the menu. "You know a bih eating for two..."

"Bih, no!" Choo-choo dared. "Who knocked you up?"

"Who else," she sighed and shook her head. The sentiment was real because not long ago she would have gladly had a child for Rue. Now it was wherever medical waste goes. "Rue punk ass?"

"Do he know?" Choo-choo asked and scrunched her face since he hadn't mentioned it to her.

"No. Cuz I'm not sure if I'm finna keep it. He kilt my granny," she said and that part was genuine as well.

"Hmp," her so-called friend huffed. Lil Baby knew she had sowed a seed so she switched the subject.

"I'm finna get the oysters gurl!" she decided. Her friend got the same and they ate and gossiped until it was time to go.

"I'll see you later gurl," Choo-choo said and looked for the car shown on the Uber app. She saw the car she arrived in since Rue was parked up the street. Lil Baby couldn't see him but felt his presence when she stepped outside.

"Ok gurl. Call me later," she said and hugged her neck. Then got into her car and drove straight to the nearest police station. She wasn't sure if one of the cars behind her contained a threat but was sure they wouldn't follow her .

"Slick ass bitch..." Rue grumbled as he drove past. He wouldn't stick around so he drove home to see what he could get out of Choo-choo. Then put the money together for the next buy, if there was one.

CHAPTER ELEVEN

"**O**h boy," Lil Baby groaned as she checked herself in the mirror before her date. She looked good in the short dress and high sandals. Good but too good for a first date so she quickly changed into a pair of skin tight jeans and even tighter T-shirt.

She and Baws had traded texts for a while then moved on to phone calls. He was intrigued by the girl but he was just means to an end. She asked loaded questions to gather information about his business since she needed leverage for her plans to take over.

"Gurl!" she fussed at herself and stopped fussing over herself in the mirror. She looked better than any of the rats who were hanging around Baws in the club so she grabbed her gun and purse before heading out.

Stepping outside was always a moment of truth. Rue was out there, somewhere and she would never be able to rest until he was resting in peace. Or better yet pieces in the bottom of an alligator's belly. Or pig shit, either way she needed him dead. Baws was bait so she wiggled over to her car to go put him on her hook.

"Sheesh..." Lil Baby winced as she entered her native ninth ward. She had grown up here but things seemed so foreign to her now. The junkies had changed places and faces since they were replaced by the next generation of lost souls.

She made her way to the spot he invited her to and parked. It never dawned on her that it was the same spot her sister Buella once killed two girls in front of. It too had changed since Baws now owned the joint. Several men milled about out front and checked her out as she walked in.

"Y'all want a picture? It lasts longer..." she fussed at the gawkers and stepped inside. Baws was working his phone as usual but stopped and stood when he saw her walk in.

"Let me hit you back," he told the person on the other line and clicked off. "Sup lil mama?"

"Lil Baby, thank you very much," she quipped but had to admit he was even cuter in the light of day.

"Yeah, I heard," he laughed.

"What you heard!" Lil Baby reeled and put a hand on her curvy hip. She knew her reputation was fully intact since she had only been with one person in her life. And he would be dead soon so he wouldn't be saying much.

"Nothing bad. All good in fact," he nodded and directed her to sit. He raised his hand and the pretty waitress was by his side before he got it fully extended. "You hungry?"

"I could eat..." she replied while watching the girl watch her. Lil Baby could tell he smashed in the past by how she looked her over.

"Brang her a basket of tenders," Baws ordered for her and the girl rushed off to fill the order.

"How do you know I like chicken tenders?" Lil Baby dared and cocked her head.

"Cuz, who doesn't?" he laughed.

"I know that's right!" she laughed along with him. The ice was broken so she got down to business. "I can beat whatever prices you paying."

"For chicken tenders?" Baws asked seriously. He was cuter than he was smart but he would do.

"No, not for dang chicken tenders!" she snickered and shook her head. "Look, you know who my people is. Or was. I got the wheel now and..."

"And the enemy of yo enemy is yo friend?" he dared. Now he cocked his head, daring her to deny it.

"Ion know what you and my ex got going on. He is my ex, as in exed out. Now, you tryna make some money or nah?" she shot back.

"I'm tryna make love," he shot back and cracked a smile that got him plenty sex in his own lifetime.

"I'm talking business and you talking 'bout some twat!" she fussed and stood but the food came. "Those do look good tho..."

"Mmhm," Baws laughed and watched her eat. His head nodded as she passed his test. "So, I'm listening."

"Like I said. I can beat whatever prices you pay now. Steady supply and..." she explained but paused to take another bite. "These are good!"

"Told you," he laughed.

"Oh, you can keep doing what you do. Ain't no more Family!" she offered and sealed the deal. She finished her meal and stood. Baws looked confused when she extended her hand.

"Oh, ok den," he laughed and stood as well. They locked eyes and shook hands to seal the deal. Now that the business was done they could get personal.

"Now, Mr enemy of my enemy," she said and tilted her head. "You tryna be my friend or naw?"

"I'm tryna be yo friend," he nodded and cracked that smile again. It had gotten him plenty of pussy in the past and looked like it would get him some more in the near future. The question wasn't if she would fuck him, it was when.

~

L il Baby felt right at home when she entered the food court of the mall. A heavy sigh escaped her throat as the good times came rushing back. Her mouth tilted into a crooked smile as she heard Jernika's voice cackling at one of Choo-choo's jokes. Then recalled Pattycake shaking her head at someone and fussing about something.

The Hot-gurls had some good times right here in this same spot. She wondered what happened that they were mostly dead and scattered. Of course she would never figure it out since she would have to accept that it was her. She was what happened and now the girls were destroyed. Just as her mentor and grandmother had destroyed so many lives before.

"Tuh," the selfish young woman huffed and shrugged and ordered a smoothie for the wait. As usual she arrived ahead of schedule to make sure she wasn't set up. She turned to head to a central table and ran smack dab into a familiar face. "What are you doing here?"

"What do you think?" Rue dared. His eyes dropped to her hard stomach and answered the question she hadn't asked Choo-choo. She had to tell him which explained how she was dripped in designer labels. She resisted the urge to pull out her gun and air the mall out. Then bit her tongue against saying that she knew he was seeing her so-called friend. Now the ball was in her court and she had the advantage.

"Hmp," she huffed since she wasn't surprised. Truth be told he was the best dealer in the Family so it made business sense that Tony kept him around. He was worth more alive than dead at the moment.

He followed her to the table she selected and locked in on her backside. It brought back memories and hopes of making new ones. Especially if she was pregnant with his kid. They sat opposite from each other while she scanned the mall for Tony. He was trained by her grandmother as well and would be early too.

"Still mad at me?" Rue offered and tilted his head.

"Nigga, you make it sound like you fucking came home late! You killed my granny!" she fussed louder than intended. Heads turned but she glared around and turned them back.

"Now see, technically I saved her," he nodded with himself. Lil Baby grimaced like something stunk but finally faced him. "That bitch Jazzy-belle had the drop on her. Put the beam right on her face..."

Lil Baby was forced to replay the horrific night once more. Rue kept nodding along with her as she remembered Jazzy-belle dropping bodies all around. She indeed had the drop on her grandmother. Big Mama had frozen in place and braced to meet her maker.

"Un-huh, you see it..." Rue coached the memory along. "She was dead anyway. So why not get my get back and kill the bitch who came to kill her? She kilt yo friends. Shit, how many times she tried to get at you..."

"You..." Lil Baby began but was interrupted when Tony traipsed along.

"Shit Rue! I told yo ass to fall back and wait!" he fussed.

"Shit woadie I'm spending big on this drop. I needs to ride shotgun with it," he shot back. Lil Baby looked back and forth between the two men as they debated. She saw through the facade and peeped the animosity. Both were a means to an end for the other which meant they would kill each other as soon as they didn't need each other. Lil Baby tucked that tidbit of info away with the rest and butted in.

"Ok, so I laid out my terms," she reminded Tony, then reiterated for the newcomer. "Half. I want half of all the proceeds."

"Three!" Rue demanded, meaning thirds. "We can split it three ways!"

Tony turned to see what she said. He hoped he had laid the pipe deep enough to make a deal. Lil Baby looked like she was considering the proposal. Her head tilted, eyes looked up and away while she pondered. Both men looked hopeful until she spoke and dashed their hopes onto the ragged shore like a shipwreck.

"Naw, half," she shrugged and smiled. "And ifn you keep following me I'ma make it sixty, forty. My way!"

"Ion be..." Rue began but realized the futility. Her evasive actions showed she knew she was being followed. Besides, he had an ace in the hole since Choo-choo was on his team. She would eventually find out where she stayed. "A'ight, don't shoot my shit up again either then!"

"Deal," Lil Baby agreed but crossed her fingers under the table. "Well, we're ready," Tony announced since the money was counted and bagged.

"We going with you tho. That's a lot of money..." Rue was saying but Lil Baby began to stand. She saw his eyes drop to her stomach once more. The baby was long gone but she could use it as bait.

"No deal," she quickly remarked as she stood and placed her hand onto her stomach. It only protruded because of the lunch she just ate. "Stop trying me. There's a reason why none of y'all don't know who the connect is. Not even Juice."

"She's right," Tony sighed and looked at Rue.

"Man," he fussed and conceded as well. It took money to make money so he was investing his own money into the buy as well. Now he could kill Tony and get back with Lil Baby. They could rule this city like they once planned.

CHAPTER TWELVE

"Send her in," Vishnu ordered. He was so curious about the call that he decided to take the meeting.

"Hello Mr Vishnu. Remember me? Big, um Eleanor's granddaughter," Lil Baby asked as she entered the room. She had been in this same room a few times while the man made large scale drug deals with her grandmother. He called Big Mama by her government name so she did too. As many times as she had been here she never uttered a word. Until now.

"Of course I do. I'm sorry I couldn't attend the funeral but..." he offered and left the explanation in the air. His relationship with Big Mama was business, not personal so there was no need to see her off.

"Yeah, I understand," she replied even though she didn't.

"How can I help you?" the man asked with a strained expression on his face. He'd hope she wasn't here for money since why would he give her any.

"The same as always. My granny brung me here to meet you for when, for in case she, you know," she stammered. "Died. So I could keep it going."

"You?" Vishnu wondered since he knew a kid when he saw one. "What about Miss Ethyl?"

"She's um..." Lil Baby began. Now it was her turn to wonder since she wasn't sure how to play this part. Her head lifted and out came the truth. "She's dead too."

"Hmp?" Vishnu nodded at the revelation. Not that he cared about internal strife or who lived or died. All that mattered to him was the money. "You have the money? A quarter million?"

"Half," she replied and saw his face change. He was all about the money so she expounded. "I have half a million. I want to double what my granny used to do."

"Nice," he nodded along. He had ten thousand dollars in cash pulled to give to the girl along with orders never to come here again. Both would remain in his pocket since he decided to do business with her.

"Same place. Same way," he ordered and nodded to Big Red. She remembered the large man with the ruddy complexion that led to his moniker. He was the one who picked up the money from the Family in one location and delivered the product in another.

"Same place, same way," Lil Baby cheesed and stood. She walked stiffly from the house and made it to her car before shouting. "Yes!"

That part of the deal was done but now she had to deal with the devil. She pulled out her business phone and made a business call. The recipient answered his business phone on the first ring since he was anticipating this call. The stash house was empty and the traps were diluting their last batches.

"So?" Tony asked enthusiastically. He wrung his hands together and began to pace.

"So he agreed to work with me. Me," she reiterated and waited for him to acknowledge.

"You, ok," he agreed. At this point he didn't care if Santa Claus was bringing the heroin. He just needed it as soon as possible.

"Except, he doubled the price. We need half a mil ifn we finna shop with him..." she relayed and waited in the silence that came. She could practically hear the theme song from Jeopardy playing in Tony's head while he did the math.

Double meant paying the same thing the various connects around the city were charging. Except at half the quality at best since it would be stepped on. There's a difference between a common connect and the plug. Lil Baby wanted to be the plug and let them control the streets. This was because she got hers off the top since she didn't trust them.

Tony did the math and it was still mathing. They tripled what they bought by adding generous amounts of cut to the product. Then charged triple what they paid for it. Even splitting it fifty/fifty he still stood to make a killing. Especially since her half would be half of a half at best. Until he could find the connect. Then this girl would be.

Tony tried to negotiate but negotiations weren't open.

"A'ight I'm finna go," Lil Baby shrugged and clicked off. She looked at the screen and watched Tony's number pop back in. "If you don't got it I'll work with Baws."

"I can get it. I'll get it!" Tony assured. He knew exactly where to get the extra money so now he clicked off to make a call.

~

"This bitch playing us," Rue grumbled as he came off the extra money to make the buy. He still stood to make a tidy profit but greed had him twisting inside.

"Of course she is," Tony replied quickly since he had come to the same conclusion. He called around and everyone else went up on their prices as well. Especially since the Family once shut them out with better product at lower prices. "We may hafta off the hoe."

"Can't just yet," Rue sighed since he thought she was pregnant with his child. He would rather get her back and kill Tony.

"Well, we need to find the plug. Then we can just go around this bitch," Tony sighed and grabbed the extra money.

"Yeah," Rue replied and parted with the extra cash. It was an invest-ment in his future but still hurt to part with.

"Let me drop this off to this bitch," Tony sighed. He missed Rue flinch since he didn't want to hear him referring to his future baby mama as a bitch.

"Where?" he asked in hopes of following.

"That much I can't tell you," Tony flatly declined. He planned to take Rue out to the swamp house one day but he wouldn't be coming back. The men nodded their goodbye and parted ways.

Rue fought the urge to follow but stayed put. Good thing too since Tony would introduce him to Bella if he did. Instead he made his rounds around town and checks the trap houses. The money would dwindle to a drip if they didn't get a new supply quickly .

Tony didn't expect to see anyone when he arrived in New Iberia and didn't. He didn't find the usual dank from the houses being closed so he knew someone had been there recently. His eyes gravitated to the rings on the floor and shook his head.

"That was a sick bitch..." he recalled from the horror stories he'd heard about the place. He looked over at the sliding door to nowhere and felt a shiver. On a quiet night you can almost hear the songs of lost souls blending into the medley of swamp creatures. Another shiver ran through his body so he put the bag down and beat it out of there. Lil Baby would come in the next day or so to collect it and make the buy.

"Mmhm..." Lil Baby hummed from her spot as she watched Tony

pull away. The buy was tonight so she came to collect the cash. She headed back down the same dirt road and went to grab the bag. Her phone rang as she reached for it and almost got ignored. She didn't though, and took her sister's call. "Yes Buella?"

"Don't yes Buella me!" Buella laughed at her tone. She had given up on her sister once before but wouldn't give up on her again. She heard something in her voice and asked, "What are you doing? Where are you?"

"Huh?" Lil Baby asked to answer the questions she didn't want to ask. "Who?"

"Girl..." Buella sighed and shook her head. "Anyway, are you ready?"

"Mmhm," Lil Baby laughed as she picked up the heavy bag of money. She was ready to make some free money since she was now the connect. Vishnu's price remained the same but doubling meant she had extra.

"Agatha, whatever you're doing, stop. Just jump in your car and come," Buella pleaded so hard it squeezed a tear from her eye. "I can't lose you too!"

"You not finna lose me!" the stubborn teen shot back. She was out of her league and dealing with killers who would kill her a hundred times over for what was in the bag. The weight of the bag stole her attention as she headed to the car. She could head north with a half million dollars and start a new life. Or she could go through with the deal and make an easy million. "I got business to tend to."

"Agatha I..." Buella was saying until she realized she was off the line. A deep sigh escaped her chest and she tossed the phone aside.

So did Lil Baby as she rode back down the same dirt road. She kept checking her mirrors to make sure she wasn't followed. A series of unnecessary turns ensured that she wasn't and she pulled into the same motor lodge she had accompanied her grandmother to. The door was opened on the first knock.

"Come on in..." Big Red ordered and stepped aside so she could. He looked down at the small girl and shook his head.

"What?" she asked when she saw it. "It's all here!"

"Not the money. What are you doing?" he asked like he was concerned.

"Uh, buying drugs," she quipped sarcastically, yet proving his point. He urged Vishnu not to do business with the kid since he knew she was in over her head. Mainly because he didn't want to have to kill her if something went wrong. He would snap her little neck on command but wouldn't feel good about it.

"This is a man's game. You should stay in your place!" Big Red barked and picked up the bag. He seemed to weigh it in his hand and nodded. It would be counted twice once he got home but it felt right so he turned to leave. "The other place, tomorrow..."

"You don't tell me what to do!" Lil Baby fussed but only after the man had gotten back into his car and pulled away. This time tomorrow she would have millions of dollars worth of dope and would run this city.

~

Lil Baby once again proved that she was in over her head when she arrived at the stash house alone to collect the product. Even Big Mama brought Buck or Juice along when she met with the man. She didn't have either or anyone she could trust so she tucked a gun in her purse and headed over.

No one outside of Big Mama's inner circle knew of this location and none of them was alive anymore. This was from where they supplied the other stash houses that Tony knew about. Had he known about this one it could have slipped to Rue who would have robbed it. The door-bell chimed and she headed over and smiled at the man in the Amazon delivery uniform.

"Don't you look the part!" Lil Baby smiled as she opened the door for Big Red. He didn't smile much in general but especially at this kid.

"I said what I said," he barked gruffly and dragged the first box into the house. A few trips later and she was in the room with millions of dollars worth of dope. What she couldn't count was the death and destruction that came along with it. People would have to die and families would have to grieve for her to succeed. Big Redd knew that and could see it in her eyes, she wasn't ready.

"Well, let's get it!" she sighed and got down to work. Luckily she dressed down for the occasion since she would work up a sweat. Even luckier was the secure packaging the dope came in because she didn't know any better than to handle it bare faced and bare handed. The heroin was pure and uncut which meant it would have seeped into her pores and addicted her through touch.

She used a calculator and made her calculations to the penny. Now it was time to load up and head out. That meant getting cute and doing some shopping. An hour later she was sashaying her cute ass through her favorite mall until she reached a familiar face.

"Well..." Tony asked when Lil Baby arrived at the food court. He twisted his lips at the shopping bags in her hands. They were supposed to be here to make a drop but it looked like she was shopping again.

"Well what?" she asked sarcastically since she knew exactly what he was talking about. She gave him specific instructions not to bring Rue but looked around for him anyway.

"He's not here," he assured and pressed the issue. "What's up with the work? We're just about out!"

"Everything is everything..." she smiled and nodded down at the various bags. The designer labels meant nothing since each one was filled with one hundred percent pure heroin. A smile began to spread on his face when he could almost smell the drugs. It didn't spread far since this was no near what they had paid for.

"Where's the rest?" he asked and looked around. He spotted Rue looking back even though Lil Baby overlooked him and didn't see him. Tony's head nodded as he answered his own question. "At the spot?"

"Yeah..." she replied and waited for the smile to begin to spread once again. Just so she could knock it off his mouth. "The new spot tho. I'll feed you when you feed me. Pay to play."

"Is that what you think this is? Play? A game..." he asked and Lil Baby finally realized he could be dangerous. So could she though so she didn't let off the gas.

"I saw my big sister in the morgue, missing half her face. Saw my granny shot down in front my face. Naw, this ain't no game and I ain't fucking playing! That's good for two hundred racks my way. Holla when you got my money and I'll feed you some more!"

"I, I, you..." Tony stammered but she was gone. He was stuck in place even after her round ass shifted completely out of sight. He was still stuck when Rue arrived at his side.

"The fuck is that?" Rue barked when he saw the bags from the various stores. He knew Lil Baby well enough to know those were her stores.

"Bitch finna spoon feed us," Tony sighed. It was enough heroin to make their investments back but he didn't like being handled, especially by a girl.

"Tole you let me take the lead on this woadie," Rue shook his head. He knew if he could get in between him and her there would be no need for him. Then it would be just him and her.

"May have to let you. If you can find out where she got the work then..." Tony sighed again and went mute since he wouldn't have much need for either if he had the work.

CHAPTER THIRTEEN

"Who stays here?" Lil Baby asked when she stepped into the well appointed house in the middle of the hood. She expected a sparsely furnished trap or stash house but this had all the comforts of home.

"Me," Baws replied and stepped aside so she could enter. It served another purpose since he got a good look at the ass from up close. He bit his bottom lip and shook his head at how perfectly round it was in the designer sweatpants.

"Wow," she reeled but it had nothing to do with the fancy furnishings. What amazed her is that he shit where he ate because she was taught to never do business where you lay your head. There was never anything more than some legal guns inside Big Mama's house. No money, no drugs in case the cops came knocking.

"Let's see what you got chere..." Baws hummed and inspected the package Lil Baby brought to him. She watched him take it into the kitchen and place it on the counter. "First things, first..."

She blinked and watched as he donned protective gear to protect himself from the deadly drug. Two pairs of latex gloves on each hand as well as N-95 mask and goggles. He pulled out his scales and grinders so he could get down to work. The tacit lesson made her step back so she wouldn't inhale anything.

"Mmhm, sho nuff!" Baws cheered when the police grade field test showed the purity of the dope. He set out cutting and testing the product as he went along. True to her word he was able to dilute it several times over and still had a better bag than anything on the streets. "They finna go crazy over this in the country!"

"Well, keep up cuz I'm rolling," Lil Baby bragged and watched as he came out of the protective gear.

"That's not a question lil mama," he replied and laughed as she twisted her face at being called out of her name. "Yeah, yeah, Lil Baby. So when you finna let me eat you out?"

"Did you say, take me out to eat?" she corrected and tilted her head for clarification.

"We can do that too," he laughed. "Now that our business is done, let's get personal?"

"Sure, I'd love to go out to dinner with you!" Lil Baby laughed. "I'll see you tonight."

"See me tonight where?" he called after her as she left the house. He wouldn't have heard her reply over all that ass shaking but she didn't.

"I'll hit you from the restaurant. Show up..." she teased and pulled away. A smile spread on her face at the bewildered look on his handsome face. Once again she was over her head since she was smiling at the devil and didn't even know.

～

"**M**mph!" Choo-choo hummed excitedly as she multitasked. She was simultaneously scrolling her timeline while delivering a blow job. Hence the humming since she had a mouthful.

"What's that lil mama?" Rue asked while he multitasked as well. As in trading text messages with the various trap houses while getting his dick sucked. Business was booming and they would run through the dope in a matter of days. Still, he stopped to smell the roses or get some head since that's important too.

"Yo gurl on a date..." she replied and turned the screen so he could see.

Lil Baby was posting pictures of her and Baws in a fancy French quarter restaurant. She would take them down soon after but knew her page was monitored. Choo-choo always dropped a like or comment and Rue accidentally liked a picture and she saw it before he took it back.

"Hur-up..." he ordered and gripped the back of her head to hurry her up. He concentrated on the task at hand and rolled off the bed.

"You need me to do something?" Choo-choo asked, ready to betray her friend on command.

"Keep it hot..." he replied and reached between her legs to fondle

72

her box as he pulled his tennis shoes on. He sucked the moisture from
his fingertips, grabbed a gun and headed out.

~

"All this fancy, fu-fu shit!" Baws laughed at the unfamiliar
environment. He was making a fortune in the drug game but
had no knowledge of much beyond the hood.

"I'm a fancy girl," Lil Baby reminded and flipped her bouncy curls.
Baws's thick lips spread in appreciation since he did appreciate the
change from his normal hood rats.

"Hors d'oeuvres..." the waiter announced with a slight curtsey as he
placed the plates on the table.

"Bruh, don't disrespect my lady! I'll slap the shit out cha!" Baws
growled and lifted a hand to do just that.

"It means appetizer!" Lil Baby interjected before he ruined the
dinner. "It's French!"

"Oh!" Baws laughed heartily while the waiter tried to figure out
what just happened. "I thought the nigga was slick dissing..."

"Merci..." she smiled and dismissed him. The smile widened when
she registered him sticking up for her honor. That was just what she
needed in her life. She quickly discovered it wasn't the only thing she
needed in her life when Baws picked up one of the raw oysters from
the ice.

He squeezed a little lemon before locking eyes with Lil Baby and
slurping the shellfish down his throat without chewing. Lil Baby
recalled the offer to eat her out and felt her box jump and quiver below.
He laced the next one up and fed it to her across the table.

"Bitch got my baby in her and eating out a nigga hand..." Rue
growled when he watched from the doorway. His presence drew a few
eyes so he backed out of the restaurant before the couple saw him.

"Mmhm, fu-fu huh!" Lil Baby laughed as the thug across the table
scarfed down different foods he never tried before.

"This shit fiyah right chere!" he had to admit. He should have left
well enough alone since he liked it well enough but asked, "What is it?"

"They call it escargot," Lil Baby smiled and waited until he had
another one in his mouth. "But really they're just snails..."

"Say what?" Baws asked and suddenly stopped chewing.

"Mmhm, snails!" she laughed. The joke was on her though since he
swallowed it down and popped another one into his mouth.

"Shits good tho," he shrugged and polished them off.

Dinner was good but the conversation was even better. Lil Baby acknowledged he wasn't just a means to an end, he was also pretty funny. She laughed and posted while Rue stewed and brewed outside.

"Joke finna be on y'all tho," Rue rumbled when Lil Baby lolled her head in laughter. He had never heard her laugh like that with him but only because he wasn't funny.

He found Lil Baby's car and discretely placed the GPS tracker under the bumper. It would lead him not only to the stash house but more importantly, where she laid her head. It was a good plan but would have to wait since Lil Baby was laying her head somewhere else tonight.

Rue stewed when he saw them walk out hand in hand. Baws said something that nodded her head before he led her to his own car instead of her own. It was her consent and she confirmed it once more when he opened the passenger door for her to sit. She spread her legs wide and looked into his eyes as he held the door open. He tried to maintain eye contact but the gravitational pull of her pussy pulled his eyes smack dab between her legs.

"Sho nuff!" he remarked when he witnessed the wet spot appear in her panties. He ran around the car and dove behind the wheel.

"You stupid!" she chuckled from her seat as he sped off towards his house. Then reached over and pulled his free hand between her legs. "Sssss!"

"Shit!" Baws exclaimed when she soaked his fingers. Her attempt to placate him so he would slow down only backfired when she bust a nut on his fingers. His foot mashed the gas until he barreled up into his driveway.

Rue fought the urge not to pull in behind them and murder them both on the spot. He needed the whereabouts of the work so he refrained and pulled down to the corner to park. He tucked his gun and crept back up the block to investigate. There's an old saying about being careful what you ask, because you might not like the answer.

Obviously the same could apply to looking into people's windows because Rue sure didn't like what he saw. The couple couldn't even make it to the bedroom since Lil Baby was leaned back on the sofa with her legs held high by the ankles. Baws rotated his whole head as he vigorously lapped at her labia. The nut she bust in the car was nothing compared to the one she let go of on his tongue.

'Grrrr...' Rue growled as he watched her shiver and shake from the orgasm. He never got that out of her but then again he didn't eat pussy.

Lil Baby stripped the rest of her clothes off while Baws went for seconds. She would have gladly come for a third time but needed him inside of her urgently. Rue was fuming when he saw Baws stand and drop his pants. He didn't want to look at the next man's dick but did since it was sticking straight out in front of him. When he wriggled it inside of her he had seen all he could and walked off.

"Fuck me!" Echoed in his head as he walked back to his car.

"Say woadie," a junkie greeted and scratched the track marks on his arm.

"Fuck outa here!" Rue barked from his broken heart.

"Let me hole a little sum," the man pleaded and grabbed his arm. A wicked smile spread on Rue's face along with his reply.

"Hole these..." he grunted and pumped several rounds into his torso. The dead junkie fell into the gutter as Rue got back into his car and chirped away.

"Don't worry 'bout dat..." Baws said as he long stroked his guest on his sofa. Lil Baby flinched when she heard the gunshots but as he explained, "They be shooting 'round here all the time..."

Lil Baby nodded and let him continue digging her out like he was looking for gold. He found it too when she came once more. Then tossed her over his shoulder and carted her off to his bedroom to search for more gold.

CHAPTER FOURTEEN

"Whew," Lil Baby had to admit once Baws dropped her back off at her car. He knocked her boots to Bogotá and back but she still wouldn't let him drive her home. She took the long way, made longer by unnecessary turns and detours just to make sure she wasn't followed. She wasn't but it wasn't needed since the GPS tracker led Rue straight to her building.

What started out as a plan to draw Rue into the open had morphed into something more the more he made her come. Baws fingered, licked and stroked her to orgasms all night and one for the road just before they got on the road. The goofy girl had learned nothing from the lessons in her life and had his DNA squishing around inside of her now. He smashed raw all night and never pulled out. She had a slight limp from the sex as she entered her building and didn't feel the eyes on her backside.

"Hmp," Rue hummed at the waterfront high rise. It was only half the battle since she could live in any one of the many units. He had no idea how he could find out which one she lived in until a familiar face happened by. He squinted to make sure but it still didn't make sense so he asked. "Jewel? What are you doing over here?"

"Tricking, duh," the girl shot back since he should know since he had tricked off with her a few times. She worked with Katie which was a connection to Lil Baby.

"With who?" he dared and tilted his head like he was jealous.

"That old white man in dere. The manager. He finna suck my pussy for a hour and fuck me for two seconds," Jewel laughed. In Mr Shein's defense the girl had some really good pussy and most men didn't last very long in it.

"Shole nuff," Rue nodded and had an idea. "You wanna make some money?"

Jewel twisted her lips sarcastically at the silly question. If she was here to fuck some old white man for money then there wasn't much she wouldn't do. Her head nodded along with the instructions, then out came her palm for the money he mentioned.

"Information first..." he said and flashed the cash as incentive.

"Say less..." she and said less herself. She marched in and straight for Mr Shein's office off the lobby.

"Well hello there Miss uh, Jewel!" Mr Shein greeted cheerfully. And what's not to be cheerful about since he was about to get some pussy. He moved over to the sofa where they usually made their usual transactions. Jewel was paid by Katie but he always gave her a generous tip.

"I need to know what apartment my friend is staying in. Ag, um..." she began but forgot the name just that quickly. Rue knew her biggest asset was her big ass so he took the liberty of writing down the name. Reading wasn't a strong point either so she sounded it out. "Ag-a-th, th, tha. Agatha Fon, I ain't trying to say this dang name! This ain't no spelling Z!"

"Spelling Z?" he asked since he'd never heard of such a thing. No one had since it wasn't a thing but he did know the name. "I don't have a resident by that name."

"I'm finna go then," she dared as instructed and turned for the door. She didn't make it one step before he changed his mind.

"I'm really not supposed to do this!" he admitted but his tongue was hard so he did it anyway. He scribbled her apartment number and reached for her hand. "Only since you guys are friends...."

"Ok den..." Jewel pouted as if she were doing him a favor. When in fact he was doing the favor since no one else would eat the high mileage vagina. She stepped out of her sweatpants and panties just before he dove tongue first between her legs. She gripped the back of his head and pulled him so deep into her muff that his glasses fogged up.

True to form he sucked her box for over fifty minutes and sucked down the juices. His time was almost up so he whipped out his tiny pink penis and shoved it inside of her. He was looking down and missed the eye roll. He had to lean to one side to get some friction since she had more pussy than he had dick.

Jewel began to count when he took his first hump. Thirty rapid fire humps later he howled and went stiff inside the girl. She shoved him out and reached for her clothes. A shower would be in order but she had another appointment in a few. Another old Zionist who loved to suck black pussy as much as they liked stealing other people's land.

"Here you go sweetie," he huffed as he tried to catch his breath.

"Thanks," she said and plucked the tip from his wrinkled fingers. She chucked the peace sign over her shoulders and headed back outside. She looked to where she left Rue but found the spot empty. He couldn't stay in one place so he pulled up from the other direction.

"Here you go sweetie," she said and produced the same paper he had given her. She added the apartment number and prepared to hand it back. But only halfway since he owed her for it.

"Here lil mama," Rue sighed and parted with a stack of fives and ones that looked like more money than it was. He snatched the paper from her hand and pulled away. The GPS tracker was still in place so now all he had to do was wait.

~

"**D**amn!" Tony cheered after hanging up with Rue. The brief drought increased the demand for the dope and they ran through the first drop in weeks.

"Yeah," Rue grunted with far less enthusiasm. He had made his investment back and everything else would be profit. He was making more money now than ever before but still wasn't happy.

In fact he was hopping mad since the GPS tracker showed Lil Baby was spending more and more time over at Baws's house. Which meant Baws was spending more and more time inside of her. The thought of the man's dick tapping his baby on the head inside her belly made his blood boil. Which was exactly what she wanted.

"We need to find that stash!" Tony reiterated once again and snapped him from his funk.

"Yeah," he repeated and resumed counting the money they owed to the boss. Neither was ready to admit it but Lil Baby was the boss. What they didn't acknowledge was that even taking half was better than the salary Big Mama used to pay them. Now they were profit sharing but both too greedy to realize. Too proud to work for a girl.

"Thought you was fucking the gal?" Tony said and pulled Rue back from his thoughts once more. "Word is, that young nigga Baws laying some grade A pipe! Plus getting all the money in the rest of the state!"

"That nigga finna get a second line fucking with me! I'ma put that boy in the dirt!" Rue growled which was exactly what the older man wanted. Rue was concerned with individual battles but Tony was trying to win the war.

"Bet that lil bitch got some good pussy too!" Tony grunted and shook his head. He missed the dangerous glare Rue shot his way. It was just a matter of time before he could carry out his takeover.

"It's all here. Call that bitch up..." he sighed and put his money back in the bag.

"Yeah," Tony agreed and made the call.

"Hello?" Lil Baby asked when she answered, even though she knew exactly who was calling. She only dealt with Tony so he was the only one who called.

"We ready," he reported and shook his head. "Same place?"

"Absolutely not," she laughed. She kept a careful eye on the car wash attendant who was vacuuming her interior since they like to lift whatever they found. "I'll hit you in a few and let you know."

"Ok, I.. " Tony replied but she had hung up. He wouldn't let Rue know he got chumped off so he kept on talking. "Ok so yeah, just hit me up and I'll meet you."

"Go 'head and handle that. I got some rounds to make," Rue remarked and left the house. The re-up meant she was headed for the stash house which meant the beginning of the end. Meanwhile her vehicle was sparkling clean and ready to go. The car wash attendant came over to hand her the keys as well as a little something extra.

"Excuse me miss lady," he announced as she looked into her purse for his tip.

"Here you go," Lil Baby said and came out with a hundred dollar bill. That's when she noticed the device in his hand. "The hell is that?"

"A GPS tracker. Yo man must think you creeping," he offered since he found them all the time.

"My man..." she wondered and shook her head. Baws was hood through and through and wouldn't know how to track it. Rue came to mind but she couldn't figure out when he could have placed it. Choo-choo came to mind but she made a box of rocks look like Einstein.

"Want me to chuck it?" he offered and broke her train of thought.

"Huh? Um..." she hummed and decided. "Nah, put it back..."

$\sim$

" All there," Tony proclaimed as he produced the bags of cash in the same place as before. "And I thought you said a new spot?"

"Changed my mind," she shrugged and looked around. Tony knew who she was looking for but let her look. She now understood why she felt could feel Rue's presence everywhere she went.

"Where's the stuff?" he asked when her survey brought her back to him across the table.

"Not here. Once I count this up," she replied and stood. His mouth opened to complain but she ran the show. She loved the money as much as he did so he assured him, "It'll be today..."

"Better be today!" Tony mumbled at her back as she walked away. There was nothing he could do except wait so that's what he did. Curiosity made him pull his phone and make a call.

'Pssss' Rue hissed when he saw the name on his screen. He didn't appreciate being left out of the loop but found something else to keep him busy. The car ahead of him pulled into a driveway but he kept on going. He slowed to crawl and watch his prey exit the vehicle and head for the door.

Rue made a quick u-turn to head back up the block and passed by the house just as a pretty, yellow woman pulled the door open. She got prettier and yellower when she beamed brightly and jumped into Baws's arms.

"I see what's going on," Rue nodded as the door closed behind them. He made one more u-turn and pulled behind the car. He watched his watch and timed it perfectly. He certainly knew what he would do with a pretty, yellow thing like that.

He wasn't wrong since the woman led her guest to her bedroom and lifted her sundress over her fine, yellow frame. Her guest stripped as she positioned herself in the middle of her bed. Her yellow legs spread as he crawled between them like a sniper looking to make a perfect shot. Instead the perfect pussy swelled and bloomed just before his eyes. It puckered for a kiss so he kissed it.

'Sssss,' the yellow woman hissed and arched her back completely off the bed. He gripped her hips and twirled her tongue around and inside of her.

"Oooh boy, you finna make, me, come!" she proclaimed and did just that. He clamped down on her throbbing box and drank from the tap. Her hips were still writhing when he got up on his knees to deliver the dick.

"My turn," he eagerly announced and positioned his dick against her slippery lips. All he had to do was push but the noise of the door being kicked in spun him around. His eyes shot down to where his gun lay helplessly in his pants.

"Got caught lacking," Rue explained and upped his weapon. One tug on the trigger splattered Baws's brains all over the pretty woman.

"I ain't seen nothing! I don't see nothing!" she pleaded with her eyes shut tighter than a child pretending to be asleep when a parent peeps into their bedroom.

Rue pointed his gun at her pretty, yellow face Blu had a change of his black heart. He had what he came for so he turned to leave. The woman kept her eyes closed long after he pulled away. It wasn't until the brain matter and blood grew cold that she rolled out from under him and called the cops.

Rue was all smiles as he pulled from the murder scene. He remembered the call he ignored and returned it as he turned the corner.

"We good?" he asked since he was supposed to pick up the work.

"Should be. Yeah," he stammered since he didn't want to admit being played by the girl. "Be on point. She's going to the stash today!"

"I'm on it!" Rue said and checked the app. A smile spread on his face when he registered the out of the way house she made the quick stop at. He now had the location which meant he no longer needed the man. Add in killing his competition and today was turning out to be a pretty good day.

CHAPTER FIFTEEN

"Um, hello! This is your..." Lil Baby barked into the phone but stopped short of giving herself a title. Baws was making good money and laying even better pipe but that didn't make her his boss or girlfriend. She was his connect though so she went there. "I've been calling you all day! I got that for you. Hit me back."

Lil Baby tossed the phone into the passenger seat and groaned as she pulled up to her destination. The children playing under watchful eyes of their parents made a perfect drop spot. She had called Tony before trying Baws again so he was on his way. She had been calling him all day but his phone was in a bag on detective Larue's desk.

She went into her head and ran through the list of chicks she knew Baws dealt with. He was supposed to be a means to an end but she was catching feelings. Not to mention his network throughout the state was moving just as much as the now defunct Family was moving in the city. A knock on her window snapped her from her thoughts and she upped her gun to the glass in the blink of an eye.

"Whoa Lil Baby!" Tony reeled and raised his hands in surrender. "Don't shoot me..."

"My bad," she said but didn't lower the weapon. She looked around for Rue but didn't expect to see him since she didn't feel his presence. She hadn't seen or heard from him in days which was more alarming than seeing or hearing from him.

"Here you go," she sighed and popped the trunk. Tony wasted no time and rushed back to collect the shoe boxes filled with heroin. Her eyes drifted back over to the kids playing. Their happy squeals and laughter broke her heart. Her father never pushed her in a swing, nor had her mother hovered near with snacks and juice boxes.

"We good," Tony announced and appeared at her window again. She was just as startled as the first time but didn't raise her gun from her lap.

"Um, ok," she sighed and put her car in gear. Tony had to jump out of the way as she absentmindedly backed out of the parking spot. She fought the urge but lost the battle and called Baws once more.

"Yes?" a woman asked as she answered. Lil Baby twisted her whole face at the woman answering his phone since she never did.

"Where is Donald!" she shot back, using his government name like women do when you're in trouble.

"He's downtown right now. Can you come for him?" Detective Larue answered and asked this time. Lil Baby twisted her face and tried to place the familiar voice but couldn't. She looked into the empty back seat and nodded her head. There was no dope or money so she agreed.

"Sure. Gimme the addy..." she replied.

"Chile I'm forty nine years old. I don't speak that!" the cop laughed at the slang. Lil Baby explained and she rattled off the address.

A sinking feeling sunk into Lil Baby's heart when she reached the address she was given. She had been here more than anyone her age should have had to. She had to identify her sister and grandmother in this same building but headed inside hoping for a different result.

"Oh lawd..." Detective Larue groaned when she saw the face she knew all too well entering the lobby. Lil Baby blinked and put her face with the voice on the phone. She wanted to turn around and walk back out but was stuck in her place. "Was Donald your boyfriend?"

"Was?" she asked since speaking of him in past tense could only mean one of two things. Either he had broken up with her or he was stretched out the back. She was smart enough to know which one it was but still wasn't sure of his title. "Was..."

"Chile you playing with some heavy dudes!" the cop barked and pulled her along by her arm. Lil Baby made no attempt to resist and limply followed her down the hall. The woman had raised her kids but women never stop being mothers even when the kid isn't their kid. "You in over yo head chile!"

The cop pulled her into the room filled with the empty shells of former mothers, fathers, children and boyfriends. This was the newest shell so it was on the slab waiting for examination. Lil Baby felt her knees buckle when she saw what was left of Baws.

"Shit!" she grunted and nearly went down. The detective held her up to make sure she saw what was left of her whoever he was to her. Or better yet, what missing since the bullet entered the back of his head and tore his forehead completely off when it came out the front.

"This is the type of people you are dealing with chile!" Larue barked and snatched her across the room. They stopped at an empty slab that wouldn't be empty for long in a city like this. Or any city for that matter since the world went crazy. They sing about murder in all the rap songs which would keep the morgues filled. "This is yours girl! You may climb up here now if you keep going the way you're going!"

"Yeah..." Lil Baby had to agree as the memories of this room came rushing back. She would jump in her car and drive straight to Atlanta but her pride got in the way. "Or, I'ma fill some of these slabs with whoever tries me!"

"Or, I'ma do to you what I didn't do to yo granny and put yo ass in jail!" Larue called after her as she stormed off.

"Ain't but two ways out of this game! Dead or in jail!" Lil Baby spat back like her granny used to say. It made less sense saying it to a cop in the morgue but she was right.

~

"Mmhm. Un-huh. Gurl!" Lil Baby grunted in reply to whatever Choo-choo was babbling about in the passenger seat. She hardly paid attention but was waiting for the inevitable question.

"Where are we going?" Choo-choo finally asked as the city of New Orleans got further behind them.

"To see Bella," she replied, since she didn't like to lie. Killing she didn't mind too much but no one likes a liar.

"Oh, ok," the girl agreed and went back to yapping about clothes, shoes, music and the rest of the bullshit that brainwashed her generation. The popular culture turned them into mental mutes while filling the pockets of their puppet masters but that's another story for another time. In the meantime they turned onto a dirt road that got the goofy girl's attention. "Who stays here?"

"No one really..." Lil Baby replied and reflected. It was certainly the truth since no one actually lived there and you certainly couldn't stay there. They reached the house over the swamp and came to a stop. "Come on."

"I'll stay here. That place looks creepy," Choo-choo grimaced as if she could hear the lost souls crying out from the swamp.

"It is creepy but come on," Lil Baby demanded. She almost pulled her gun but thought of a better weapon and smiled. "Let's smoke one."

"You?" she reeled since the girl never smoked or drank with them.

The promise of free weed couldn't be ignored so she hopped out and was by her side.

"Gurl yeah!" Lil Baby fawned and opened the door. She was used to the smell of the blood and misery spilled inside since bleach can't remove it.

"Ain't even no furniture in here! Where..." Choo-choo began but a hard right hook to her head interrupted her and sent her reeling. "The fuck!"

"The fuck is you fucking my ex!" Lil Baby shot and shot a jab right into her mouth.

"We finna fight over a nigga you ain't want?" Choo-choo shot back and put up her fist to do just that.

"Naw, we fighting over you being a snake!" she declared and attacked. Choo-choo could fight just as well so they beat on each other while talking. "You put that thang on my car?"

"What thang?" Choo-choo asked in between giving and taking blows. Choo-choo couldn't spell GPS but it didn't matter now.

"You told that nigga my business!" Lil Baby growled and dipped under right and left hooks. She was low enough so she swooped in and scooped the girl off of her feet. Choo-choo felt her feet leave the ground and braced herself for impact.

"Ugh!" Choo-choo grunted when she was slammed on her back. The impact knocked the wind from her lungs and left her stunned. That was just the advantage Lil Baby needed.

"Un-huh..." Lil Baby hummed as she climbed on top of her old friend. She pinned Choo-choo's arms at her sides using her body weight. Then used both hands to pound the girl's face until she looked different. A tooth fell out of her bloody mouth and both eyes were swollen shut.

"I'm sorry..." Choo-choo managed before going out. Had Lil Baby continued she would have beat her to death. The words stopped the pounding and she stood.

"I forgive you gurl," she sighed and shook her head. Lil Baby stepped from the beaten girl and opened the door to nowhere. Then came back over and rolled Choo-choo to the exit.

The black swamp below churned in anticipation and they would not be disappointed. Lil Baby used her foot to roll her old friend into her watery grave. The initial splash was followed by fierce splashing as the creatures scrambled for a bite. "Forgive, but not forget. Don't worry, I'm finna send you some company..."

$\sim$

86

"Sup woadie," Rue greeted happily when he stepped inside the house. Getting more dope to make more money always made him giddy. Killing Baws put a little extra pep in his step.

"You did that shit?" Tony asked since news of the murder had spread quickly.

"Did what?" he asked but the smirk on his face told the truth. "All I know is I'm finna take the market out in the country."

"Hmp?" Tony huffed since that wasn't a bad idea. Whoever took up where Baws left off would make a killing and probably get killed as well. "We finna be ready to re-up soon."

"Then we wait on ole gurl to see the connect. Catch her while she got the whole bag," Rue nodded as if he included Tony in the plan. In the meanwhile he needed Tony to give him his product. "You got that?"

"Yeah. Bitch spoon feeding us," he lamented and passed off the dope he picked up. Rue was still the main dealer for the company which made him indispensable.

"This the last of it?" Rue asked offhandedly as he checked inside of the bag.

"Yup, we..." he was saying but the blur of Rue upping his gun stole his train of thought. Tony always expected the double cross since he planned to cross him as well. He went for his gun too but Rue had the drop on him and dropped him on the spot.

"Your services are no longer needed..." he told the corpse as he stepped over him and searched the house. Rue emptied the safe of the rest of the dope and cash. Then dug into his pockets and relieved him of the contents of his pockets.

Rue just eliminated another piece on the board and was getting closer to the queen. A few more moves and he would have checkmate.

CHAPTER SIXTEEN

"Sorry about your loss," Rue offered but the sarcastic smirk contradicted his condolences. Baws's was stretched out in the casket in front of them but the lid was closed due to the mess he made of the man.

"You did this..." Lil Baby snarled and looked around.

"Hmp," he hummed in neither an admittance or denial. "I suspect the same thang happened to ole Choo-choo?"

"Hmp," she hummed in the same fashion. "Can't bury a cum rag tho huh?"

"You shole can't," Rue shrugged since he wasn't mourning either of the newly deceased.

"Why is you here tho?" Lil Baby asked and winced as she looked around the room full of strangers. She recognized a few of Baws's workers looking confused. Most didn't know how to butter their own bread now that he was in a box. She was here to pay her respects since it was only right.

"Strictly business with me lil mama," he replied. Killing Baws was definitely personal but attending his funeral was business.

"Speaking of business?" she asked and furrowed her brow. "Where is Tony? He's not answering."

"Ion know..." Rue replied but once again the smirk contradicted him. "The money is good tho. We're gonna need to re-up soon."

"Hmp," Lil Baby hummed and turned to leave. She nodded at the box containing her ex lover and headed for the door. Rue watched the wiggle in her hips but stayed behind. Like he said, he had business.

He made it his business to push up on all the out of town dealers who were at the funeral. Most genuinely liked Baws but needed a new connect since he couldn't sell dope from the graveyard. You can only sell it until you get to it since all roads lead here.

~

Lil Baby groaned when she pulled up to her destination. Tony's car wasn't in the driveway but she still got out and headed for the door. She hadn't decided on her approach as she approached but the door opened before she could reach it.

"Where is he? What did you do to Tony?" Tony's wife demanded as she stormed out of the house. Their son came out behind her until she barked and sent him scrambling back inside. "What did you do?"

"Me? I ain't did shit to him! I'm tryna find out where he is myself!" she shot back but left out the main reason she was here. She was more concerned with the money the man owed her than the man himself.

"He told me you were a snake! You and yo rotten ass grandmother!" the woman shouted and spit at the memory of her grandmother.

"Bitch..." Lil Baby shouted and attacked. Tony's woman was a square but this was her home so she fought ferociously. She gave as much as she got but a fist fight in the quiet neighborhood didn't go unnoticed by neighbors. The sounds of sirens rang in different directions as cops converged on the scene.

"You killed him!" Tony's wife spat after her as Lil Baby tried to get to her car and get away before the cops pulled on the scene. She just managed to get behind the wheel when she was quickly surrounded by gun pointing cops. If she sneezed they would have claimed they feared for their lives and gunned her down on the spot.

"Don't shoot!" Lil Baby pleaded and raised her hands. The door was snatched open and she was quickly snatched from the driver's seat.

"What's going on here?" the sergeant on the scene asked and looked back and forth between the two women. Big Mama always taught to control the narrative anytime she could so Lil Baby spoke up first.

"Just a lil spat over a man. I be sleeping with her husband," she offered. It worked too since Tony's infuriated wife tried to get at her again while she was handcuffed.

"Lies! He hated you and yo granny! She killed him! She killed my husband!" the distraught woman shouted.

"Clear. No crime scene..." a cop announced after finding nothing in the house.

"Well..." the sergeant sighed and contemplated cutting her loose. He would have to had to, had the name not come back.

"Sarge she has a flag on her name," the cop tasked with running Lil Baby's name reported.

"Book her for disorderly conduct," he shrugged since he couldn't just let her go since she was flagged. The department that flagged her was notified and would be waiting when she reached the station.

~

"**D**ead or in jail..." detective Larue laughed as she entered the interrogation room a few hours after Lil Baby was cuffed to the desk. She shivered from the arctic cold air blowing from the vents to freeze suspects into confessions.

"Lawyer!" Lil Baby shot back and tried to prevent her teeth from chattering but couldn't.

"But, you're not under arrest yet. Which crime do you need a lawyer for?" Larue asked and tilted her head.

"I ain't did shit!" Lil Baby fussed and wrapped herself in her own arms.

"So, why is this lady in the next room telling me you killed her husband?" the cop asked.

"Cuz she found out I be fucking her husband and he be paying all my bills!" she shrugged.

"Doubt that," Larue said and pursed her lips as if it tasted like a lie. "She's telling me a bunch of stuff over here. Swamp houses, alligators..."

Lil Baby just shook her head at the pillow talking Tony must have done at home. Rue did it too after a good nut so she assumed all men did it. Women didn't so she had nothing to say. She adjusted her crossed arms and said nothing. A cop stuck his head in for attention so the detective got up and stepped out.

"Anything?" she asked hopefully since she needed something to hold her on besides the fight.

"Nothing," he sighed and shook his head. There were no drugs or guns in the car so he produced the GPS.

"One of ours?" she asked of the police grade tracker.

"No," he replied since the numbers weren't in the system.

"Hmp?" Larue wondered and thought until an idea snapped her fingers and parted her lips into a smile. "Hack it. I wanna see wherever she goes..."

The cop nodded at the way to skirt the rules. GPS trackers required court orders and probable cause. Hacking into this one would bypass all those steps and get eyes on her in real time. She waited for him to access the device and download the data before putting the device back where he found it.

"Dead or in jail," detective Larue repeated as she stepped back into the room. Lil Baby rolled her eyes defiantly so she reached over. The girl remembered the slap and flinched but the cop simply uncuffed her wrist.

"I can go?" she asked as she rubbed the mark left by the cuff.

"For now. I'll see you back here in a few or down to the morgue," the woman relied. The look in the woman's eyes froze the girl in place. Lil Baby had never seen this in her grandmother or Ethyl's eyes before. Only her dead mother the last time she saw her.

"I um, I..." Lil Baby stammered. She wanted to stay, to talk but the gravitational pull of the streets was too strong. She dropped her head and slinked out of the room.

Larue just shook her head at what she knew was coming. Hoping for the best meant putting the girl in prison for a long time. Graveyards last even longer.

~

"The fuck you been?" Rue asked when Lil Baby finally arrived at the meet.

"Huh?" she asked since there was too much noise inside of her head to hear what he was saying. The lady cop had finally broken through her thick skull and made sense. There were only two ways out and she wasn't ready for either one. If the mighty Big Mama could get touched so could a lil baby like her.

"Never mind. I need that work. I done sowed up the whole state!" he bragged, then stated his purpose. "So I can take care of you and the baby."

"Baby?" Lil Baby asked and actually looked around for this baby he spoke of. Once she saw him looking at her flat stomach she remembered. "Oh yeah! Nah, ain't no baby. Been sucked that shit out me."

There was a moment of deadly silence as they locked eyes and contemplated their next moves. Rue could kill her on the spot but needed the dope first. He had half a million dollars in cash to make the buy but the plan in his mind was priceless.

Lil Baby thought about killing him on the spot as well. She could take that half a million and drive north to Atlanta. Rue looked on curiously as she ran through various scenarios in her mind. A soft smirk pushed the corner of her mouth upward when she settled on her plan.

"I'll meet you right back here in a few," she said and spun on her heels. "Finna grab the work and be rat back..."

"I'll be right here!" Rue called after her and stayed put. For a few minutes that is since he had the GPS to follow from a distance. She made a quick stop to pull the GPS tracker off and attached it to a eighteen wheeler at the gas station. It was facing south to her north which would give her some room to maneuver.

"Shole nuff..." Rue said when the GPS passed him in the other direction. He would have made a u-turn and followed if he hadn't seen her up ahead. Now he fell back in the line of cars and followed.

"Pick up, pick up..." Lil Baby groaned as she drove and dialed. The call was answered on the first ring since she had her own ringtone.

"Agatha? Are you ok?" Buella asked urgently. The calls between them only went one way so getting a call took her breath away.

"Who? Yeah, I'm on my way up," she replied just as urgently. "Just gotta make one quick stop..."

"Girl fuck that stop! Just come!" her sister pleaded. She had no idea what she was up to but knew it was between her and her sister. "Just come!"

"I got this. I'm on my way!" Lil Baby assured and clicked off. She had another call to make so she made it.

"Hello?" detective Larue asked when she took the call she never expected to get.

"You wanna make a big bust? A major dealer in the city?" Lil Baby asked as she formulated the rest of her plan.

"I'm listening," the cop said and wrote down the details. She gave up Rue's soon to be whereabouts when she dropped the drugs off to him.

Since Tony was no longer living she moved the stash to the swamp house along with her savings. She would give Rue the dope so he could get busted and spend the next twenties years in prison. Even though she planned to spend some money and have him murdered once he got inside.

She would take her cash and go start a new life in Atlanta. The plans spread a wide smile on her face until she was pulling down the long driveway to the swamp house. The drugs were in the rarely used bedroom so she loaded them into the trunk. Then ran back inside to collect the cash from under the blood stained floorboards. Some of her father's blood was on the boards she pulled up and tossed aside. Then came up with the cash.

"Sho nuff?" a familiar voice called from behind and spun her around. Lil Baby reached for the gun in her purse but both were still in the car.

"The fuck you doing here!" she barked and balled her fist to fight to the death if need be. She had removed the tracking device when she last came here so he shouldn't know about it. Plus Tony was dead so she moved the cache of drugs out here where she stashed her money. Now he was here with everything she owned.

"Looks like I done came the fuck up!" Rue laughed and pulled his gun. "His eyes went wide at the bundles of cash she had pulled from the hole in the floor. He had generated millions in the street but seeing a million in cash made his knees buckle. Lil Baby took advantage of the moment and went for her purse since she had a gun inside it.

Rue raised the gun but couldn't shoot. Instead he socked her and sent her scrambling across the room. He was between her and the door and removed flight from the 'flight or fight' mode. With nothing left to do she put up her fist to fight.

"Sho nuff?" he laughed and tucked his gun. He was from this new generation of males who shot other males but didn't mind fighting a woman. "I've been wanting to whoop yo spoiled ass!"

"Same!" she shot back and shot him with a jab that busted his bottom lip. The sight of his own blood sent into a rage and he released a flurry of furious blows and kicks. She made matters worse by laughing as she dipped and dodged most of the blows. "You fight like Patty-cake. 'Cept she hit harder."

"Arrrrgh!" Rue shouted in a blind rage. He gladly ate the jabs and hooks she bombarded him with just to reach her. The blows were accurate but didn't phase him. Now he managed to get his hands around her neck. Once he grabbed her throat he squeezed and lifted her feet off the ground. "Un-huh, smart mouth lil bitch!"

Lil Baby tried to fight and claw to get free but fighting and clawing both require oxygen. And hers was cut off by the vice-like grip around her trachea. Her feet dangled in mid air as she began to fade. Some say their life flashes before their eyes before death but Lil Baby didn't have time. She thought of his sisters and accepted her fate. Everything went and she faded away. Her mind registered a 'bang' and thuds as she hit the floor below.

"Agatha! Agatha!" a faraway voice called but she was too far to answer. Lil Baby felt her soul leaving her body and she was ok with it. The person calling wasn't though and she kept shaking and calling. "Agatha! Come back Agatha!"

"Ugh!" Lil Baby groaned when her soul landed back into her body. That was the most peace she had since leaving the womb but now she was back. Her eyes blinked as she tried to make sense of what was happening. Death can be confusing like that.

"There you are!" Detective Larue cheered when she returned to the land of the land of the living. She stood up and let the girl process what was happening. The hole in Rue's head, lying in front of her, explained the bang she heard before going out.

"Am I going to jail?" she wondered as she sat up.

"I shot him," Larue explained, which explained the gun in her hand. They both looked at the money, then back at each other. "That's a lot of money."

"How did you find me?" Lil Baby asked to switch the subject from her money. She nearly died for it once tonight.

"GPS tracker. I downloaded the history," the cop explained and went back to the money. She had worked a lifetime and loaded her retirement funds but didn't have a million dollars.

"You can have it," Lil Baby offered if it meant not going to jail.

"What about him," Larue wondered. The dead body had a bullet from her service weapon in its head.

"Who?" Lil Baby asked with a snicker and stood. Larue didn't feel a threat and didn't raise her gun. Instead she watched as she opened the door to nowhere. The curious cop walked over and looked down to the black, churning water beneath.

"I'm not even going to ask how many of my missing people are a part of the ecosystem..." she said and shook her head.

"So, what's one more?" Lil Baby asked since she really wanted to be free. So much she sweetened the deal, "And keep the money. Just let me go."

"Go!" detective Larue blurted before she could change her mind. The million in cash could change her life so she began grabbing the bundles of cash.

Lil Baby didn't need to be told twice so she

grabbed her purse, ran out and hopped into her car. She tore down the bumpy dirt road and chirped onto the asphalt pavement. She didn't realize she was still holding her breath until she was forced to inhale.

"Fuck that money!" she reassured herself as she drove away from the house. Her brain kept telling her foot to let off the gas pedal but she needed to get away. She barely escaped with her life but was still alive and finally on her way to Atlanta. Except for a detour when the police lights flashed behind her. "Shit!"

"Do you know why I stopped you?" the cop asked after running her tags and coming u

p clean. It looked like a routine traffic stop and ticket so he pulled his pad.

"Cuz I was

speeding!" she confessed and extended her hand for the ticket.

"That was easy," the cop laughed since it was recorded on his body can. This would save him some time coming to court so he began to write it up. A fellow state trooper slowed as he passed just to make sure everything was ok. It was until the k9 in the back seat went crazy.

"Hmp?" the second cop wondered at the strange reaction and pulled over. Lil Baby just sighed at yet another delay.

"Sup Bob?" trooper one asked trooper two as he approached with the dog.

"She alerted as I passed by?" he had to ask since it didn't make much sense.

"As you passed?" the first one asked since it was a first for him as well. The dog went crazy again and began to pull towards the trunk. "Ma'am, do you have any drugs in the vehicle?"

"Drugs? No, I don't know about any drugs," she replied with a naive eye flutter.

"Ah sheeeeeee..." the second cop laughed when the dog pulled with all its might towards the trunk.

"Would you mind popping the trunk ma'am?" he asked.

"Sure!" Lil Baby offered and happily pressed the button since she never carried drugs on her. Except this time since she had put the dope in the trunk to take to Rue. "Shit!"

"Shit!" cop two reeled when he saw the kilos of dope strewn about the trunk.

"Shit!" cop one cosigned when Lil Baby attempted to turn the ignition. He dove through the open window and grabbed the keys from her. He pulled her from the car and cuffed her behind her back. "You have the right to remain silent. Anything you say..."

"Awe shit," Lil Baby sighed and shook her head because she knew exactly what this was.

~

"Your lawyer is here to see you," an officer announced as she poked her head into Lil Baby's cell.

"Bruh, why y'all ain't call the cop? Detective Larue, from New Orleans!" she pleaded just as she had from the moment she was placed under arrest. Cop one actually did make the call from the side of the road but the call got ignored. The detective had over a million dollars that she couldn't explain in her car. She took no calls and made no stops until it was safely tucked away.

"Ion know nothing 'bout all dat. Are you talking to this lawyer or not?" the country cop drawled in a country accent. Things were different out here in New Iberia than back home in New Orleans.

"What lawyer?" Lil Baby asked as she followed behind. The cop ignored that question as well and led her into the room. She stepped aside so she could enter and closed the door behind her.

"Do you remember me?" the man with the familiar face asked and answered. "Clyde Walker. I was your grandmother's attorney."

"Oh yeah!" she recalled and smiled. "Can you please get me out of here?"

"You were apprehended with a lot of narcotics. One hundred percent pure heroin," he laid out to walk the answer on like a red carpet. "You're not in the city. This is a big case out here. The biggest in the history of Iberia parish. You made history so no, I can not get you out of here."

"Did anyone call the cop? Detective Larue, she, we, I mean. Just call her!" she pleaded.

"I um know the detective very well from her dealings with your grandmother. I did in fact try to call her but she's retired," he informed.

"So what am I looking at?" Lil Baby asked and lifted her chin.

"Depends. If you cooperate and give up the supplier..." the lawyer suggested.

"I ain't no fucking rat!" Lil Baby snapped before he could even finish the offer. "I'll do a huned years cuz I ain't telling on nobody!"

"I'm glad to hear that," Mr Walker sighed in relief. He had to report back to Vishnu who had sent Big Redd to Atlanta to kidnap Buella if she cooperated with authorities. "It'll be more like twenty years tho, not a hundred."

"It's whatever!" Lil Baby said with her chest. It was

what it was and what it was, was...

The End

EPILOGUE

Lil Baby entered the courtroom and smiled at her brokenhearted sisters. They both tried and failed to save her from herself. A plea hearing still beat a wake and funeral even if she was facing twenty years. Neither sister noticed the large man with the reddish complexion sitting behind them in the courtroom.

Vishnu sent Big Redd to monitor the proceedings as well as be a deterrent against changing her mind. Lil Baby lifted her head above the threat since honor was more important. Many street dudes would snitch on their own mama to save a few years but she was here to take twenty on the chin.

The judge reluctantly accepted the terms and banged his gavel at the end of the proceedings. Lil Baby left the same courtroom as Agatha Fontenot and never went by Lil Baby again. Keeping it one hundred meant Vishnu's protection in prison instead of putting a bag on her head.

Clyde Walker finally relayed the rest of Big Mama's will and the five million dollars that came with graduation. The one stipulation was she split it with her sisters which she gladly did since she earned several degrees during her time.

Time that was cut in half since detective Larue still had some pull within the system even after retiring. She had put enough people behind bars to be able to get ten years grace for the girl she tried to save from herself. Still, this was no happy ending because too much blood had to spill for it to be happy. It was just the end.

. . .

Thanks for your support for the Lil Baby series. Continue reading this free bonus book. The first book I ever penned....

CHRONICLES OF A JUNKY

By
Sa'id Salaam

PROLOGUE

"Willie?" my mom asked from room to room in the sing song tone reserved for me, her precious, precarious three year old.

"Are you hiding from me?" she asked as her search yielded no results. "Boy where are you?"

My mother's tone went from playful to frustrated to concern when she spied the sliding glass patio door was open. Panic set in as her eyes quickly shot to the open fence that surrounded our in-ground pool.

"Willieeee!" she screamed for both me and my dad who graciously allowed me to share his name.

When my mother came into view, I was looking up from the bottom of the pool. She screamed frantically for me but my lungs were full of water so I couldn't reply.

That's when it happened. I actually left my body and began rising out of the pool. My dad passed me on the way down to retrieve my body.

I watched peacefully as I rose higher above the scene. As my dad brought me to the surface, my mom pulled my body from my father allowing him to climb from the pool.

"Call 911," he yelled, sending mom flying back to the house. I watched as my dad began chest compressions that forced the water from my lungs. Every time he pressed I seemed to descend. Finally, with one last thrust I was back in my body coughing furiously.

"Thank God!" my father exclaimed, as he pulled me into his arms. My mother, who just returned, echoed his sentiment exactly.

Even though my parents spoke of that day from time to time during my life, I did not remember it—until now—now that I'm rising above my body again.

CHAPTER ONE

My name is William Champion and I am a junky. I don't particularly like that label but I do like to get high, so it is what it is. I know the term usually elicits a dirty, run-down addict nodding on a street corner. However, I am, or at least was, the polar opposite.

I was raised in the upscale Atlanta suburb Dunwoody. My neighborhood boasted homes starting at half a mil. Most of the residents were old money. Most households had a Mercedes outside in the driveway and both parents inside.

We were no exception. My dad William Champion, Sr. grew up there attending the superior schools and connecting with future movers and shakers like himself.

After graduating from the prestigious Dunwoody Prep, he attended Atlanta Tech and excelled in its engineering department.

My father was tall and possessed the solid frame of an athlete, but never played sports. Nonetheless, he did catch the eye of a pretty co-ed I now call Mom.

My mother was from the hood. She grew up in the rough streets of Decatur, Georgia, a quaint suburb, next door to Atlanta, with an incredible murder rate. The eldest of two children, my mother's main goal was getting out of the hood. At 18 she moved into the dorms of Atlanta Tech on a full scholarship never to return...ever.

That meant leaving her younger sister, who already showed a penchant for the streets, to the streets. It was her chance and she took it.

As a result, six years later at 15, my aunt Betty gave birth to my cousin Brett, a week after I was born. Brett and I didn't get to spend a lot of time together as kids but were close nonetheless.

At times when my mom was bickering or lecturing her sister, Brett could spend nights at our house but, I was never allowed to sleep over their house.

By high school, both Brett and I were star athletes each excelling in our chosen sports.

He was hands down the best wide receiver in the state, if not the country. Me, I was the best point guard on the east coast. Although there is the possibility I could go pro, the focus was my education.

While some kids loathe to follow in a parent's footsteps, that's all I aspired to do. I intend to go to Atlanta Tech and excel at engineering, just like my dad.

Like my dad, I had my future wife secured already. Prentice and I had been groomed to be together since kindergarten. Our parents were close and arranged our marriage early. I assumed they considered their combined stock would produce healthy, good looking, high IQ grandbabies.

Prentice was prim, proper and very sadity. Her long brown hair was augmented with streaks of blonde that perfectly framed her pretty face. She, of course, is a virgin which makes me one too.

Being a star athlete, I get hit on a lot but I'm dating the head cheerleader so I decline all offers. Even if it means settling for the occasional hand job I can beg her out of every once in a while.

My cousin Brett on the other hand has fucked half the girls in Decatur. He sent pictures to my e-mail of all kinds of girls doing all kinds of stuff. Sometimes I have to give myself a hand job after looking at all that.

Since our parents couldn't come together and organize a graduation cookout, we had them back to back.

Mine of course was a catered affair, complete with tents and fountains set up in our back yard. Everyone chatted in quiet little groups, while the live band played soft rock hits from the 80's.

Everyone was properly dressed – men in chinos and polos, women in long flowing sundresses.

"Say Shawty, dat fuck nigga tried to card me to get a drank!" Brett fumed when he returned from the bar.

"All they have is white wine anyway," I offered as consolation.

"Good thang I brought my loud pack," he said, producing a nearly rolled blunt.

"Dude, my mom would absolutely lose her mind if you lit that," I said near panic.

"Chill Shawty," Brett laughed, "I see it ain't that type of party. Come thru tomorrow and we finna do it up."

"Roger that," I agreed as hiply as I could. Guess not hip enough because my cousin laughed as he went to his car.

CHAPTER TWO

"Sessalie, that boy is 18 years old," I heard my father say in my defense, "just graduated and has been away for weeks at a time. What's the big deal about spending a night at your sister's house?"

"First," my mom began, in her attempt to forbid me from sleeping over after Brett's cookout, "my sister is ghetto. She will not supervise the kids."

"OK and so what? They'll have fun?" My dad chuckled.

"You don't understand that neighborhood, those people," my mom sighed.

"Those people? Black people? Your sister?" my dad asked before putting his foot down. "Tell him *WE* said it's fine."

"OK," mom said, ever the obedient wife, "but mark my words, he'll never be the same."

"Yessss!!!" I said, pumping a fist as I eavesdropped.

I hurried down the hall and ducked into my room before my mother came out. After a laundry list of do's and don'ts she shared what I already knew. I could spend the night in 'da hood'.

Bret's BBQ was held in an alternative universe than the one I hosted the day before. Dudes all had on baggy shorts pulled down to expose their boxers and over half were shirtless; and the girls...oh...my... God! They were naked. Cleavage and ass cheeks everywhere. I made an appointment with myself for a hand job as soon as the party was over. If I made it that long.

There were no caterers fussing about, just Brett on the grill, and beer runs. Feeling a little, well a lot out of my element I stuck close to Brett and took it all in.

"Hey baby," a tall Tyra Banks looking stallion sang and gave my cousin a juicy kiss.

"What's good shawty," Brett drawled as soon as her tongue cleared his mouth. "Dis my cuzn Willie, Willie dis my gal Tonya."

"Pleased to meet you Tonya," I said, extending my hand.

"Hey Willie," Tonya managed between chuckles, "dis my gurl Mel."

I turned to speak to her friend but got stuck. Standing before me was a chocolate colored girl who made time stop. She wore a mesh dress that left nothing to the imagination. My dick got so hard, so quick, I nearly fainted.

"You aight cuzn?" Brett asked as my knees buckled.

After I got myself together, the four of us kicked it. I politely declined all offers of weed and alcohol. Mel flirted non-stop the whole time.

It was near midnight when the inevitable fight broke out. After all the liquor, weed, and chicken, all that was left was a fight.

Two guys went at it pretty good while their cliques looked on. I was scared to death, but my cousin never even looked up from the grill.

Once the gladiators finished beating on each other, the party resumed, as if the fracas never happened.

"Shawty digging you cuz," Brett announced as he took the last of the meat off the grill.

"Who?" I asked, even though I should have known better. Mel had been staring at me since she arrived.

I realized hood chicks are far more aggressive than the girls in my universe. She been licking her lips and blowing me kisses all night.

"Who you think nigga?" My cousin chuckled, "She done set the ass out for you. All you gotta do is take it."

"Cuzo you know I'm in a committed relationship with Prentice," I replied, sounding corny even to myself.

"Nigga, you in the presence of a stone cold freak and you talking shit about a chick who won't even let you touch the pussy," Brett said, walking into the house.

I again surveyed my surroundings with amazement. These kids were my age and younger but everyone, everyone was both smoking weed and drinking.

I'm not sure what propelled me to the cooler but there I went. I extracted an ice cold beer and opened it. My first sip of beer caused me to frown from the bitterness. The second was a gulp and the next finished the green bottle.

Eager to catch up with everyone else, I pulled another one out the ice and cracked it.

"Not you cuz," Brett laughed, returning from inside.

"I guess you was right, it ain't gone kill me," I replied, showing off the ebonics I'd just learned.

"Say yall," Bret announced loudly, "party ova! You ain't gotta go home but you gotta get the fuck outa here!"

It took a few minutes for the crowd to exit the backyard. When the last person left, Brett, Tonya, Mel and myself settled into the den.

"I'm finna put in a movie," Mel said, bending over to make a selection. When she bent over, her ass strained against the mesh giving a clear shot of how well developed she was.

"You aight ova dere cuzn?" Bret laughed, seeing my reaction.

"Yeah I'm cool," I replied, glad they couldn't see the real reaction straining my pants to be set free.

"Smoke one?" Tonya asked, huddling up close to Brett.

"Shit, I been on dat grill all day. Yall do it," he said, tossing a bag of weed on the table.

It looked more like green popcorn to me as I inspected it. The girls looked at me as if I was expected to roll the blunt but I wouldn't know where to begin.

"I got it," Mel announced, grabbing the weed off the table.

I got another erection when she slid her tongue around the cigar to moisten it. I watched in fascination as she split the cigar with a pinky nail, then dumped the guts on the table.

She crumbled up a good amount of the fluffy weed and tucked it inside. When she re-rolled it using her saliva to seal it, I made up my mind to try it. I wanted to be anywhere her tongue had been.

I was already feeling the mellow effects of my first beer when I took my first pull off my first blunt. By the time a full rotation had been completed, I was good and high and I loved it!

Tonya and Brett were making out pretty good, so it was no surprise when they got up and rushed from the room.

"So what's up?" Mel said, seductively sliding closer.

"With what?" I stammered.

"I'm saying," she replied and kissed me. It was the first time I'd kissed anyone other than Prentice or my mom, and neither of them used their tongue. Mel ran her hands over my body as we kissed, until stumbling upon the wood.

"Damn Boy!" she exclaimed because of how hard I was.

It felt so good to be out of the confines of my pants when she pulled my dick out, but then she worked her hand better than Prentice or I ever did.

She pulled my shirt off and sucked my nipples and chest, as I fought not to cum. I recalled the last hand job Prentice gave me months back, and how she flipped when a little cum got on her hand.

I then experienced a sensation like I could never have dreamed. *Nah, it can't be,* I said to myself before looking down. When I did, I saw Mel had half of my dick in her mouth and I exploded.

"Mmm," Mel moaned, milking my dick with her hand. At that moment, I decided to skip school, leave Prentice, run away and just stay right here...inside her mouth.

Mel went and got us another beer. When she came back in the den, she slipped her dress off, slid her thong to the side and straddled me. As much as I wanted to fuck her, my body wasn't ready yet. We shared the beer, as we licked and sucked on each other's naked bodies.

She smiled when she felt me rise again. She lined me up with her vagina and wriggled me inside. A condom crossed my mind but the weed and alcohol said it would be OK without one. She slid slowly down my rock hard dick and by the time she reached the bottom, I came again!

"Dang boy," Mel chuckled, "I know I got some good pussy but let me get a nut too!"

"I'm sorry" was all I could think of to say in my moment of satisfaction.

We took a break to smoke another blunt, then went at it some more. She showed me positions I didn't think possible. I calmed down enough for her to begin riding me. Although the effects of the beer and her riding me had me feeling a little weird, I didn't want it to end. This time I managed to control my excitement for about 10 minutes and then she made us both cum. Mel sexed me for the rest of the night.

Looking back on that night of many firsts I'd have to say, that's what turned me out...Did me in. Too many pleasures at once.

Over the course of the summer I was so busy with basketball camps and orientation that I didn't indulge in anymore sex or drugs, but I thought about them both everyday.

CHAPTER THREE

Since Brett had a scholarship to Atlanta Tech as well, my dad let us use his condo downtown. While most kids dealt with musty dorms, we had it made.

The condo was an investment property my dad purchased years back and had quadrupled in value since. We were living in luxury.

I began smoking weed again, every chance I got. I saw Mel every chance I got. She and Tonya would come spend the night a couple times a week. Brett had a few more girls but I was content with Mel.

My cousin had been selling weed all summer and kept the best weed in the house. Everyday it's kush, or dro, or purp.

I was living a double life. There was William, the star athlete/honor student, and cool Will who drank and smoked a little. I enjoyed being Will more and more by the day.

Brett's weed business was obviously doing well, based on the new Lexus he came home with. It was the same model as mine. Only differences was the color and source of income to pay for it. Mine was a graduation present from my parents. The streets paid for his.

We started hitting the strip clubs pretty regularly and got carte blanche everywhere we went. I tried my best to be faithful to Prentice's hand but my cousin brings home two or three, sometimes four women every night.

One night, we brought a couple of strippers home from the club. Destiny and Unique proved there is a God. They were perfect! Perfect face, teeth, eyes, breasts, ass...just perfect.

As soon as Brett spotted them he offered to pay them for the night, if they left with us. I couldn't hear the negotiations but we all left together.

I had since learned to roll a decent blunt and did so while Brett went to his room. He came back a few minutes later and handed Unique a plastic bag of white powder.

"Heeeyyy! That's what I'm talking about!" she exclaimed happily.

Let's get this party started!" Destiny announced.

I watched in awe as the two perfect women made perfect little lines on the glass table. Destiny rolled a dollar bill and snorted two long lines up her perfect nose.

"What's that?" I asked anxiously as she fell back in ecstasy.

"Don't tell me you ain't never seen no powder honey!" Unique chuckled before mimicking Destiny.

"You studying that shit kinda hard," Brett said harshly, noticing my gaze never left the pile of cocaine on the table.

"Huh? Oh naw I'm cool," I replied, even though I still hadn't looked away from the drugs on the table.

I inhaled deeply on the blunt, secretly wishing I could try the shiny white powder

The girls snorted, drank and smoked until all stimulants had been exhausted.

Well let's get to it!" Brett announced with a hand clap.

"Y'all want us to dance?" Destiny asked, as she rubbed her nose.

"Naw I'm tryna fuck something," he replied, grabbing Unique's hand.

"That's what's up! This blow got me horny," she replied as he led her from the room.

"Well?" Destiny asked as soon as were alone. I took the hint and led her to my bedroom.

"Nice!" she exclaimed at the luxury I took for granted.

As she entered, she began to undress. By the time she reached her bra and panties, I was in my boxers.

"Damn!" Destiny laughed, grabbing my rock hard dick. "You betta not cum all quick. I'm tryna get mines too!"

"OK," was all I could think to say.

"Here," she said, digging into her purse. "Take a bump. It'll make that thang stay hard."

I complied willingly. She lifted a pinky nail loaded with coke. I inhaled the two scoops she offered and felt its effects instantly.

My mind, body and soul went numb. Destiny was right, I stayed hard all night and punished her. The cocaine coursing through my system made me feel like Superman.

The next morning after we dropped the girls off, Brett and I stopped for breakfast. We ordered our food and waited silently for it to arrive.

"Say cuz, what was that about last night?" I finally asked.

"Yeah, I was trippin Shawty," he offered by way of an apology. "I just don't really like them coke hoes. Can't trust 'em."

"I feel you," I said, not feeling him at all. Destiny was cool and the sex was ridiculous! "That girl got some fire head...almost as good as Mel!"

"One I had too! Suck the skin off a dick," Brett laughed. "Speaking of Mel I heard she on the blow too. That's why Tonya don't fuck with her no more."

That explained why I hadn't seen or heard from Mel lately, even though Tonya frequents the apartment. We went on to fill each other in on the night's freaky festivities. I chose not to talk about the blow.

CHAPTER FOUR

Months had passed before I next saw some cocaine. I was hanging out with our power forward, Al, after a game. Al is from Spanish Harlem, the east coast coke capitol. After a stellar performance with him going for 30 points and 19 boards, along with my 28 points and 15 assists, it was only right we celebrated.

"You fuck with this yo?" Al asked in his 100 mile an hour New York accent, sounding like Damon Dash.

"No doubt," I said eagerly as my mouth watered at the sight of the coke.

He dumped out what appeared to be three times what the strippers had on the table and began making lines.

I lit a blunt and watched as he used his bank card to chop the drug and make snortable lines.

"Argh!" Al exclaimed after running a line in each nostril and then falling back on the sofa to enjoy the sensation. "Here B," he said, handing me the rolled bill for use as a straw. "Careful yo that's that raw. Ain't that cut up shit y'all got down here.

I had no idea what all that meant but found out quickly.

"What the world," I said after snorting my lines. The powerful drug invaded my senses before I straightened up from the table.

My whole being went numb. I felt like Super Fucking Man—probably could leap a tall building right now.

"Uh huh! Told ya ass," Al laughed as I sank into euphoria.

We smoked, snorted and drank for a couple of hours before Al suggested hitting a club. We took his car even though I'm almost sure I could have flown.

Being star athletes, we got star treatment at the club. I would have been cool to stay in the trenches where the action was but we were whisked into V.I.P. upon entering.

I could still feel and taste the cocaine draining from my nose into my throat. When the champagne arrived I gulped it down.

"The fuck yo!" Al uttered and took off.

He's back in a flash with two of Georgia's finest peaches. Typical ATL chicks—thick, pretty, and underdressed.

"Ayo dis Star," Al said, wrapping his arm around her exposed waist. "An Tyra," he said shoving the other towards me.

"What's good ma?" I said in my fake 'up-top' accent.

"Oh lawd! Another damn Yankee," Tyra exclaimed.

"Nah shawty I'm skrate out dat Dec.," I shot back in yet another phony accent.

The girls joined us in the booth and helped us empty a few more champagne bottles. All the while I was still sniffling and rubbing my nose.

"Say shawty what's up with that salt?" Tyra leaned in and asked. "Can I get down?"

"Ayo son," I laughed to Al, "let's bounce B."

I was relieved not to see Brett's car when we got back to the condo. I had plans on snorting a few more lines and wasn't feeling hearing his mouth.

"Damn! We done came up on some ballers!" Star shamelessly exclaimed upon entering.

"I know," Tyra co-signed. "Member dem broke ass niggas that took us home last week?"

"Um hmm," Star frowned. "Nigga apartment all empty, tryna fuck. I was like hurry up and nut so I can go home."

The freak alarm went off and me and Al smiled at each other. It was about to go down.

"So um...what's good then?" Al said, taking off his shirt.

The girls stood and stripped off their clothes in response. For the next few hours we engaged in an orgy taking breaks only to snort more coke and drink champagne.

Again, drugs went hand in hand with incredible pleasure. In my mind, the two were linked. I didn't want to have sex without being high and if I got high, I wanted to fuck something.

Al and I began to hang out on a regular basis and my drug use increased. As a result, I began to slack off in other areas of my life.

A lot of the extra training I used to do was a memory. I blew off practice at times and skipped meetings. I was still putting up big numbers so I wasn't worried about the complaints.

CHAPTER FIVE

B ret usually kept a candy bowl full of weed in the den to accommodate us. One day I came in and to my dismay, I found it empty.

I was near panic as I dialed his cell phone.

"What's good cuz?"

"Cool, cool, where's it at? The weed? Ain't no weed?" I asked, hearing the desperation in my voice. "The bowl is empty!"

"My bad cuz. I meant to fill it up 'fore I left," he said before telling me that he and Tonya had went down to Albany for the weekend.

"Look Shawty my safe ain't locked, get you some weed but don't mind that other stuff in there," he said.

I can't even recall if I said goodbye before hanging up and tearing off to his room. I was propelled by my need to get high and my curiosity as to what *that other stuff* was.

"Jackpot!!!" my mind screamed when I saw a sandwich bag filled with large chunks of cocaine. I filled up the candy bowl with weed and broke off a good size chunk of coke.

After smoking and snorting alone, I was ready for some company. Mel didn't answer and neither did Tyra. The next time I opened my eyes I was seated in the rear of a strip club.

In the darkness, I snorted cocaine scoping out which dancer would fulfill my needs.

"Wanna dance?" A short, thick and obviously young dancer asked.

"I'm tryna fuck something!" I said boldly. Even I heard the change in me. The Willie Champion I grew up as would never say such a thing.

"It's two hundred for V.I.P. and you gotta give me two hundred too," the young girl instructed.

She led the way upstairs to where the private rooms were located. After paying the bouncer, we entered and took a seat.

"I don't suck no dick," the stripper announced matter of factly as she extended her hand for payment.

I paid her and stripped off my clothes. Since she was almost naked already, it took no time for her to join me.

As soon as she rolled a condom on me, my dick fell limply to the side. Hard as I tried, I could not manage to get an erection.

"You got another hundred?" she asked kneeling in front of me.

"Sure do," I said, reaching for my pants. I figure her remark about not giving head was a sales pitch. No sooner then her fingers clasped the bill, her lips clutched my manhood.

In no time I was fully erect, as the young girl worked her neck. I felt the urge to protest when she climbed on top of me and slid down my raw wood. Here I was having unprotected sex with a nameless stripper. How many times had she done this tonight? How many men? The drugs in my system combined with the sights, sounds and pleasure of this young girl overwhelmed me. I slammed into her until I released pent up frustrations inside of her.

On the drive home I thought about my own recklessness. "Fucking a stripper raw! Must be on drugs!" I said out loud, laughing crazily.

I waited for Bret to say something about the missing cocaine when he came home but he never did. I was ready to pay for what I took but he obviously didn't miss it. Curiosity finally got the best of me. "Say cuz, what was up with that blow you had in the safe?" I inquired. "Thought you said you hate that shit."

"I hate being around people who use it, fucking junkies Shawty. Can't trust 'em," he exclaimed.

My paranoia suggested he meant me but still I fought the urge to confess.

"I've been making a few moves here and there but that country ass town Tonya from is a gold mine!" he added, excitedly.

"Oh, that's why you down there every weekend?" I asked, catching on.

"Shit dem country niggas pay three times what I get up here," he bragged.

"Put me down," I urged, eager to get some disposable income to dispose of.

"You?" Brett laughed. "Nigga you already rich! Uncle Willie got you straight."

He was right about my being straight but my new lifestyle was getting expensive.

"Speak of the devil," Brett announced, looking at the display on his vibrating cell phone. "Dis dem country niggas now. What it do?" he drawled to his Albany customer.

From my end I could ascertain another deal was scheduled for the next weekend.

"That's what's up," he smiled before hanging up. "Dem niggas gone make me rich! They stepping up to four ways now."

"A four way?" I inquired, naively.

"Yeah, four ounces instead of the one or two they been copping. I'ma hit dem for like five stacks!"

I made up my mind then to stay out of his stash. I had no idea that stuff was that much money. I can't afford it.

CHAPTER SIX

Once basketball season ended Al and I hung out daily. He always had good coke and I would supply the smoke and drink.

Every night was strip clubs and a parade of strippers or loose girls from regular clubs.

One night Al came to scoop me to hang out and hit a few clubs. "What's up B?" he asked cheerfully, upon entering the condo.

"Chillin B," I shot back in my mock 'up-top' accent.

"Ayo, see if cuzo got some blow. My peeps was dead," he said eagerly.

"Shit! Brett went out of town," I sighed woefully.

"He ain't leave nothing?" Al asked with a tinge of desperation in his voice.

For a reply I shot into his room and checked the stash. To my delight there was a nice size bag of white powder.

Then I remembered Brett saying it was accounted for so anything I took would be missed.

"Yes and no," I told Al upon my return. "I think that's for someone."

"Shit, we'll just take a little and put some cut on it," he exclaimed.

"Cut?" I asked eagerly. The idea of getting high had me open for anything.

"Yeah, he ain't got no cut?" Al asked, sending me back into Brett's room.

"I ain't seen nothing," I said, feeling dejected.

"Come on," Al exclaimed, grabbing his keys off the table.

A few moments later we pulled into a nearby head shop. I always thought it was only a freaky sex shop but it carried a full supply of drug paraphernalia.

"Let's get this cuz that milk sugar makes you shit," Al explained as we surveyed the selection behind the counter.

As we browsed, a small white man waited sheepishly behind us.

"Ayo son, go 'head," Al ordered. "We gone be a sec."

He walked around us and approached the counter hesitantly. His nervous demeanor caught both of our attention. He held his hand by his side as he made a selection.

"Rough Rider lube," he said meekly to the multi spiked, multi tatted, multi pierced clerk.

"Speak up," the clerk demanded curtly.

"Eh em I... um... I need the Rough Rider lube," the little man repeated.

"Anal lube?" the clerk questioned amused and amusing us.

"Yes please and um this too please," he said, placing a rather large dildo on the counter.

I instantly hit the floor rolling in laughter.

"What the fuck is that?" Al exclaimed to the now red faced customer. Once he realized what it was he joined me on the floor in the throes of laughter. The store clerk chuckled too as he completed the transaction. The poor fellow paid for his new friend and scurried off to fuck himself.

We ended up buying a four ounce bottle of cut and a small digital scale. When we got back we swapped out three grams of pure coke with 3 grams of the cut.

After a few lines and blunts, we were ready to hit the streets of Atlanta. Before we did, we swapped another 3 grams.

Over the next few months I regularly swapped out pure cocaine for cut. Since Brett never mentioned it I kept on doing it.

CHAPTER SEVEN

Rico and Tavarious were two of Albany Georgia's up and coming dealers. They had been dealing with my cousin Brett for a year and getting good money.

About the same time I discovered cut, their product had become increasingly weaker.

"Dis shit fucked up too," Rico lamented when he finished cooking up what should have been four ounces of coke.

"How bad this time?" Tavarious asked with a scowl.

"Damn near a whole ounce!" Rico spat.

"Dis fuck ass nigga tryin us," Tavarious growled, "Playin us like some Bamas."

"I know if this next one short, I'ma see bout dis nigga," Rico said, patting his nine millimeter pistol for emphasis.

Thanks to me their next package of 4.5 ounces was 3.3 oz of coke and the rest milk sugar.

When their cook up came up short they didn't complain, nor did they ask for a refund. Instead they placed their largest order yet, a half a key.

"Say cuz, take a ride down to the country wit me," Brett asked as I walked into the condo.

"Man I would ride out with you, but Prentice in town," I half whined. Brett always tells me about how fine and freaky the country girls were and I was dying to sample, but I knew I had to be neglecting my lady. I planned to spend a whole sober, sexless weekend with Prentice.

"Aight Shawty! I'm tryna put you on with Big Bertha! Suck an egg through a garden hose and not break the shell," he laughed.

"I have no idea what that means," I laughed, eager to find out.

"Shit cuz, we ain't hung out in forever," Brett said genuinely.

"He was right too...with my hanging out with Al in the clubs, Brett and I only saw each other coming or going.

"We gone kick it when you get back. That's on everything. I'ma take you out," I offered sincerely.

"Shawty I'm finna charge dese country niggas twenty for half a block," Brett chuckled, "I'ma take you out."

We kicked it for a little while longer before he took off.

I enjoyed Prentice's presence in the condo, even though the large amount of coke I skimmed off the package my cousin left with was screaming my name.

When I had seen how much cocaine was in that bag, I made a beeline to the head shop and bought four ounces of cut. I swapped the whole thing.

A couple times when I stole a minute away from my girl, I pulled out my stash and stared at it. It took everything I had, but I didn't get high.

I resisted all temptations. My cell phone was turned off to avoid my freaks. Instead I got a couple hand jobs from Prentice as we made out.

CHAPTER EIGHT

When Prentice finally left on Sunday I wanted to rejoice. I couldn't decide what to do first. I definitely wanted to get high, and I definitely needed some pussy.

I decided to get high, then get some pussy. I pulled out my stash and dumped a few grams on the table. I put my cell phone on speaker so I could check my messges while I prepared a few lines for snorting.

As I scanned through my messages I crushed, sorted and lined up the blow. When I inhaled the first line a stoic sounding message caught my full attention.

"This is Detective Harris with the Homicide Division of the Albany Police Department. Please give us a call."

I check and rechecked the message several times, snorting lines the whole time. It was almost an hour later when I finally placed the call.

I was given the grim news that my cousin was found dead. A couple on their way to church found him slumped behind the wheel of his car.

I gave the detective my aunt's name and number to avoid having to relay the tragic news. I did however, have to drive down to ID the body and retrieve his car and personal effects.

Al took the ride down with me and halfway there I realized how close I had come to going down there with Brett. It could have been the both of us laying on a slab, waiting to shock a family member.

The grim thought pushed me to retrieve the traveling blow we brought along for the ride.

"Ayo fam, I know you shook up but you think it's a good idea to go up in there high?" Al asked hesitantly.

I simply snorted a dose in each nostril as a reply. Before I knew it, we were pulling in front of the small building that housed the police department.

"I'ma chill here," Al said as expected. I didn't want to go in there myself, so I knew he didn't want to. I was so high it felt like my feet barely touched the ground.

"Willie Champion," I said, taking the detective's outstretched hand. I was shocked that the cop looked so ordinary.

Detective Harris looked more like me than a cop. He was 25-years old at most and dressed casually.

"Nice to meet you. Sorry about the circumstances. I'm actually a fan of the both of you guys," he said warmly.

"What happened to my cousin?" I asked plainly, taking the offered seat.

"Not exactly sure," the detective admitted. "He was shot once in the back of the head and although he was discovered this morning, the M.E. puts the time of death at some time Friday night."

"Was it a robbery?" I inquired.

"Again, we're not sure. We haven't ruled that out but he still had his wallet which contained several thousand dollars, his watch and jewelry," the detective explained.

"Why would anyone just shoot cuz in his head?" I responded on the verge of tears.

"I was hoping you could help us with that?" Harris asked.

"Me?" I asked. "How can I help you?"

"Well for starters what was he doing here? Do you guys have family here?" the cop asked.

"Family nah, but his girl do. He probably was seeing them," I said, reflecting on his coke deal and knowing Tonya was back in Atlanta.

"You think drugs could be involved?" he asked as if we were cooler than we were.

"Nah, we athletes. We don't mess with no drugs," I said convincingly.

The detective stared at me momentarily as if he was trying to see if he could see the truth in my face.

"Well, thanks for coming down, once we finish processing the car you can claim it," he said, pushing a large envelope across the desk. "These are his personal effects."

I peeked in and took in the wad of cash and diamonds. Is this why my cousin died? I wondered.

The case drew national attention. A young NFL prospect being gunned down in a small town was excellent fodder. I had to turn the ringers off on the phone to avoid the onslaught of calls. Most were condolences, and some media. I was not in the mood for either.

Instead I smoked blunt after blunt from the several pounds of kush I found in Brett's room. Between the weed and alcohol, I was in a stupor.

The one call I did take further pushed me into the fog of depression engulfing me. It was Detective Harris informing me that two arrests had been made in my cousin's murder. He advised that he would fill me in when I came for Brett's now cleared vehicle.

This time Prentice took the drive south with me. We rode in virtual silence the whole trip. Once back at the police station, we met with Harris and his red neck partner Detective Ard.

"Have a seat guys. Let me fill you in," Harris said almost cheerfully. What cops don't realize is that solving a case, while pleasing to them, does nothing for the bereaved. How can there be closure on an untimely death...a murder.

"Turns out it was drug related," Ard said with a slight grin on the corners of his thin lips.

Both cops paused for a reaction from me but got none.

"So you didn't know anything about the drugs?" Harris asked, nodding.

"Nothing!" I shot back, causing Prentice to snap her head in my direction.

"Well, yesterday a known dealer by the name of Tavarious Henry was caught with two ounces of crack cocaine. Rather than face his second trafficking charge, he told on his friend," Detective Ard explained.

"Seems they had been buyings large quantities of powder cocaine from your cousin and according to Tavarious the quality went from sugar to shit.

"What does that mean?" I asked, still not up on all this slang.

"The drugs had a lot of cut in it. Rico, the alleged shooter took it personally. He felt like they were being dismissed as country boys and taken advantage of. So they placed an order and when Brett produced the dope, they checked it and again it wasn't right. Rico questioned him and your cousin denied it, saying there was no way that could be. Rico took being lied to even more personal, so he shot him in the head from that back seat. Your cousin never knew what hit him." Harris laid out.

"That explains why he still had his valuables and cash," Ard threw in.

I heard nothing afterwards. I was aware that my swapping out real drugs for cut is why my cousin was dead. I killed him myself.

After the meeting we were given Brett's keys and we left to take his car to Aunt Betty. As soon as we stepped out of the station Prentice confronted me.

"Why did you lie?" she asked with a pained expression.

"Huh? What?" I asked curtly, being snatched away from my thoughts.

"In there? When they asked about drugs? You lied!" she yelled.

"I ain't lie, I don't know nothing about no dope."

"Willie Champion, I've known you your whole life and I know when you're lying," she stated plainly.

Whatever she 'knew', she'd have to live with cause I said nothing more. I was relieved to be alone on the ride back and free from all distractions.

The only thing on my mind was getting high. I wanted some coke and that disturbed me deeply. It was at that moment I decided to leave the dope alone.

As soon as I made it back to the condo, I flushed the last of the coke down the toilet like the shit that it was. I still felt a craving as it disappeared from sight. I had to fight the urge not to fish it out. Instead I smoked a blunt in silence, preparing myself to bury my cousin the next day.

Brett's funeral was fitting for the royalty that he'd become. Everybody from sports to entertainment came to show their respect. At least half of the student body came through.

And of course the hood showed up. A parade of ballers, hustlers, pimps and hoes. I doubt if anybody got a table dance that day because all the strippers were in attendance.

My Aunt Betty was inconsolable, even though my mom and I stayed at her side. Everyone who actually knew Brett came over to offer their condolences.

As I saw Tonya approach, I did a double take at the familiar face next to her. After hugging Brett's mother, Tonya hugged me and sobbed on my shoulder. Mel was next to hug me and I got hard instantly.

I chided myself for my reaction but it was beyond my control. When I broke off the embrace I was met by Prentice's stern gaze. Mel seemed to catch it as well and retreated before we could speak.

After the funeral I went home with my parents and slept for two days. Monday morning I went to class from mom and dad's. When I finally returned to the condo the answering machine, as well as the voice mail on my abandoned cell phone, were filled to capacity.

I only half listened to all the messages of condolences not intending to reply to any of them. One message did manage to catch my full attention—it was Mel.

I immediately dialed the number she left only to get her voice mail. I tried hard not to but I still detected a sense of urgency in my tone as I left a message.

Thirty minutes later she called back and thirty minutes after that I was inside of her.

"Dang Boo," Mel said out of breath, "you ain't never gave it to me like that!"

"I just missed you is all," I replied nonchalantly.

I was proud of the pounding I gave her from my new sexual experience.

"Twist one up," I suggested, pulling out some weed. "I'll fix us some drinks."

"You mind if I roll it dirty?" Mel asked me as I left the room.

"Do what you do," I replied instead of admitting I didn't know what she meant.

Mel said she wasn't hungry, so I scarfed down a slice of pizza before returning with a bottle of wine and glasses.

When she lit the blunt it seemed to sizzle with each pull. I inhaled it deeply when she passed it and was super high by the time I exhaled.

"Fuck!!" I exclaimed at the tremendous feeling.

"I know that's right!" Mel laughed. "I ain't know you smoked primos."

"Shit's primo alright," I agreed before taking another healthy pull. I had never felt so good in my life.

After we got high we had sex again, then again, then yet again. I blew off my classes that next morning and Mel and I slept into the afternoon. A probably would have slept into the evening if Al hadn't come to get me for the team meeting.

"Damn son! Who that!" Al exclaimed as Mel sashayed out past him.

"A little something – something; you know how I do," I chuckled.

"Ma fine! What it hit like?" he asked intensively.

"Stone...cold...freak!" I exclaimed. "We smoked some primo weed and ..."

"Primo?" Al cut in.

"Yeah we smoked some weed called primo. That shit had me super high. Shit was sparking when you hit it," I said.

"Son a primo is fucking crack son!" Al said adamantly. "Woola, Jums nigga!"

I was horrified, twice. Once because I had actually smoked crack, and two because I couldn't wait to do it again. Last night I had experienced feelings I'd never felt before.

CHAPTER NINE

The rest of the semester passed quickly. And true to my word, I didn't use any more coke. Al offered whenever we hung out but I always declined.

I focused on basketball and was putting up impressive numbers that NBA scouts flocked to witness.

Prentice and I had drawn even closer over the months. My grades had picked back up and I was feeling like my old self again. I had put the Champion back in Willie.

Besides the occasional blow job by cheerleaders or team groupies, I had cut out my sexcapades as well. Life was good.

First game of the year and I was unstoppable. When it was all said and done I had 42 points, 15 assists, 10 rebounds, and 5 steals.

The rest of the season went the same way. By mid-season I was 20 points shy of the school's single season scoring record.

The hype surrounding our next game was nothing short of spectacular. I was doing interviews on TV and radio the whole week. Not only were we playing the number one ranked team, but I was assured to blow the record away.

The opening tip came to me and without hesitation I pulled up a long three that barely disturbed the net as it passed through. The crowd went wild.

My teammates were eager to see me catch the record and kept the ball in my hands. I hit five more three pointers by the end of the quarter.

"You got all game to set the record Willie," my coach advised. "How 'bout you sit for a while? Make it interesting."

Before I could object, my teammates chimed in on my behalf and I started the second quarter. To make it a little more interesting, I didn't shoot for the first few minutes.

With all the attention our opponents gave me, I easily racked up ten assists. I passed on the few open shots I did have. The record would have to be spectacular.

Finally my opportunity came. Al blocked a shot and kicked the outlet pass to me. I had a breakaway.

A million ideas flooded my mind on how I should finish. I thought about just pulling up a long three that would pass the mark rather than just catch it. Nah, if I missed that wouldn't be cool.

I decided to take off from the foul line and dunk. I adjusted my steps and prepared for flight. Something went horribly wrong.

I felt it as soon as I planted my left foot on the foul line to launch. The pain was excruciating! It felt like I had stepped on a land mine. I heard a disgusting 'pop' as my knee went out.

I collapsed under my own weight and went sliding under the goal. I grabbed my shattered knee, writhing in pain. The trainers and coaches were quickly by my side.

The looks on their faces hurt worse than the fire in my leg. The stretcher came and whisked me away.

After an eternity and a million tests later, the doctor came in with my dad in tow.

"Dad?" I questioned, sensing his presence meant disaster. The doctor looked grimly as my father stepped forward.

"Son," he began, taking my hand in his, "you know I am very proud of you. Not just your mom and me but the whole family. The whole city."

"What, am I dying or something," I laughed even though his demeanor terrified me. "Doc how bad is it?"

"Well," the doctor said after clearing his throat, "you've suffered a complete tear of your ACL and there is other collateral damage.

"OK, so what you gotta operate or something?" I asked.

"Yes we actually want to operate tomorrow to repair the damage, as best we can," he said in reply.

"OK so let's get it!" I cheered. "I can still play by tournament time!"

My dad squeezed my hand tightly as I made that statement.

"Well William, with therapy you'll walk just fine. Slight limp perhaps but uh..." the doctor paused.

"But uh what?" I pleaded becoming alarmed.

"Son, you won't be able to play again this season," Dad said, tightening his grip even more.

The doctor cleared his throat prompting my father to go on.

"Willie you can't play anymore. The damage is too extensive," he blurted painfully.

"What! What!" I said, exploding in rage. I tried to get up and go after the doctor but was restrained by my father. Oddly enough I felt relief in my rage. I just wished I could get at the doctor to satisfy the new emotion. Rage felt good.

The tears my father shed were a first for me. I'd never seen the man cry, ever. His tears summoned my own. The doctor slipped out the room as my father and I sobbed.

When I left the hospital a day after my surgery, I just wanted to be left alone. Over my parents protest, I went to the condo to recuperate. I turned off the ringers and shut down from the outside world.

A few days later, I heard the front door open and in walked Prentice.

"How'd you get in here?" I barked as she entered.

"Your mom gave me a key," she said matter of factly as she dragged in a large suitcase.

"What the hell is in there?" I demanded.

"My stuff. I'm staying with you," Prentice said defiantly.

"I'm cool so kick rocks," I said with more venom than I felt. Self loathing is best done alone and I didn't need the distraction.

"Nope, I'm not going nowhere. You can be as nasty as you like, but I'm staying," she demanded. I saw her begin to tear up and felt remorse for my behavior

"Well," I began, as if I still had the attitude, "if you're staying then you need to get over here and hold me."

With that she rushed over and embraced me.

"Watch the knee," I cautioned with a chuckle as she climbed on top of me.

"Ooh I'm sorry," she sang, kissing my face.

"Hand me my pills please?" I asked, pointing to the wonderful assortment of painkillers the doctors had given me.

The pills not only killed the pain but had me soaring. I stayed high off them, taking them even if I felt no pain.

When my supply finally ran out, I called my doctor for more. He reluctantly wrote another prescription even though by his estimation I shouldn't still be in pain. He warned that painkillers could be addictive and that this would be my last refill.

Prentice turned out to be a huge asset to me. She was prepared to drop a semester but her school rallied behind her and let her take her classes online.

She took me to and from rehab for my knee, waiting patiently. I went hard to get back in shape. In my heart I knew I was gonna play again. I intended to prove the specialist wrong.

My father didn't have much faith in my return and offered me a position in his firm. I accepted out of sheer loyalty to him, even though I knew I would play again.

Prentice believed in me and supported me to the fullest. She wasn't just my lady, but my best friend. My biggest supporter and number one fan. The time was right to show my appreciation.

The line at the Trendy eatery was long, as usual, but being a local celebrity has its advantages. Upon arrival, we were whisked inside to table. We made small talk over dinner, then ordered dessert.

On cue the wait staff brought out a huge cake ablaze with dozens of candles.

"Oh there must be some mistake it's not either of our birthdays," Prentice said when the cake was placed on our table.

"It's not a birthday cake," I smile brightly. "Read it."

"Congratulations?" she read questioning. Her face twisted with bewilderment as all four of our parents came into view.

"Willie? What's going on?" she asked almost fearfully. "Why are our parents here?"

"To witness this," I smiled, presenting her a two carat solitaire. "Prentice will you marry me?"

She of course flipped when she realized what was going on. The entire restaurant erupted in applause as I slipped the ring on her finger.

"Yes! Yes! Of course I'll marry you," she screamed, setting off another round of applause from the patrons.

CHAPTER TEN

Prentice moved into the condo and we set up house. By the end of the school year, I was done with rehab and walking fine, yet I continued with the painkillers. There was no pain to kill, I just liked the feeling they gave me. It was a functional high.

I worked at my dads firm, if you could call it work. I was in the Manager in Training Program, learning to supervise employees with tons more experience than me. He bought himself a new Mercedes and gave me his Lexus convertible.

Prentice was clerking at the Georgia Supreme Court, racking up experience for her future law career. Life was great.

A few weeks before school started back up, we had our first argument. Prentice found my supply of painkillers and had a fit.

"Why are you still taking these?" she questioned.

"Painkillers? They're for pain duh!" I replied sarcastically.

Well where are you getting them from? I know full well the doctor is no longer giving you these. I know you're not in pain anymore," she said sternly.

I watched in horror as she flushed my remaining pills down the toilet. My mind flashed back to when I flushed the last of Brett's cocaine down this same toilet a year ago.

"Happy now!" I exploded startling my soon-to-be wife.

"Willie you're acting like a junky in need of a fix," she shot back.

The remark triggered an argument which ended with me storming out of the house. Even in my fury I knew she was right. I needed a fix. I wanted to get high.

Those were the last of my pills. I'd long been cut off from my doctors and had been buying lose pills from a white guy at school, who had since been arrested.

As the withdrawal symptoms grew worse, I tried in vain to find something, anything to get high. I took a couple drags off a joint in the dorms but no one knew where to score weed.

Al's phone went straight to voice mail fifteen times in a row and I finally took the hint. My desperation led me to a number in my phone that I vowed never to call.

"Willie?" Mel questioned upon answering her phone. I hadn't seen or heard from her since the primo incident.

"Yeah, it's me. What you doing?" I inquired reluctantly. It would have been cool if she had said she was busy, or that her man was over, but instead she said she was waiting on me.

I picked up a bottle of wine and followed my GPS to Mel's apartment. My mind flashed to our last time together and I got an instant erection. I sat in my car talking myself into not touching her. I'm an almost married man. I'm here to hang out with an old friend, get a buzz. That's it!

Mel greeted me with a tight hug and wet kiss and I was hard again.

"Oh you brought me some wine!" Mel sang cheerfully as she let me in.

"Yeah, you got some weed?" I inquired as I took a seat.

"I sure do baby. I got a nice primo rolled up waiting on you," she said going for glasses.

I argued with myself about smoking primo again. Al's words came rushing back, "That's fucking crack son!"

In the end I decided a couple of pulls wouldn't hurt me. "Just a few pulls, glass of wine, home to the wife," I chanted.

Mel gave me a crooked look but it only made her pause for a minute. She didn't say anything...just resumed rolling the blunt.

I was so high after we finished the blunt and bottle, I could only watch as my dick disappeared into Mel's mouth.

During the blow job, Mel asked me if I would buy some more dope so we could smoke another one. With her tonsil massage of my manhood, of course I agreed.

Mel used a free hand to send a text message while the other stroked me. After she took me there, we lay back until her dealer came through. I paid for a fifty of hard and quarter of weed. And we alternated between drugs and sex until dawn.

I returned home to my future wife, who was unexpectedly contrite about the argument. She apologized profusely and offered some make up sex. Luckily neither of us had time before work so I asked for a rain check.

Realizing I dodged another bullet, I vowed to leave Mel and the drugs alone. For good this time.

CHAPTER ELEVEN

The season was weeks away and even though I had not been cleared by the doctors I secretly prepared myself for my comeback. Every morning I ran miles before class. Then hit the weight room at night.

"What's up champ?" Coach asked me after catching me working out.

"Season bout to start—trying to get ready," I replied.

"Well," he began stoically, "Willie you know there's always a spot on the team for you."

"A spot?" I chuckled. "I am the team!"

"Well, get cleared for practice and let's see how it goes," he offered.

I didn't get cleared to play but coach ended up letting me practice anyway.

In the off season the school had recruited a point guard from out of the Bronx named DeSean Salaam. I had to admit, the kid was good. OK, real good. He put you in the mind of Marbury with the no look passes and typical New York City ball handling skills.

Still, I'm the starting guard. The kid can either back me up or play the two. I made sure to let coach know this as well.

Coach matched us up during a scrimmage perhaps to prove a point. Somehow word got out and the bleachers were full.

Al got the tip to me and I pulled up from damn near half court. Swish!

"Nice shot!" DeSean said genuinely.

I guarded him closely as he brought the ball up until he crossed me over and disappeared. By the time I saw him again, he was at the rim finishing a pretty finger roll.

I'm not 100% and it shows. I made ten more long three's but the kid ate me alive. Made me look downright silly a few times with that fucking crossover.

"You got a nice game man," I congratulated him after the scrimmage. My 40 points and 15 assists paled in comparison to his 50 and 20.

Thanks B, that means a lot coming from you. You like my idol yo," the humble little fucker responded.

Hard as I tried not to like the kid, I did anyway.

One morning while running my knee became wobbly and it was over. This ACL tear was devoid of all the dramatics of the first...my career as a professional basketball player wasn't going to happen. This time everyone tried to console me, saying that I would and could come back but I knew it was over. I accepted defeat. There would be no NBA for me. It's over.

I recuperated after the surgery without the help of the pain pills. I did begin to smoke a little weed occasionally but that was it.

Prentice was due to start law school that summer right after graduation. I accepted a position in management with my dad and accepted my fate. And what a fate it was! I lived in a half a million dollar condo, had a great job and planned to marry my soulmate.

On the even of my wedding Al threw me a bachelor party in a rented suite. Knowing my penchant for champagne, dude had a case of the stuff. On the table was a mound of weed and an ominous pile of white powder.

"Is that what I think it is?" I asked bewildered.

"Nigga don't act all brand new," he laughed. "Tonight's the last night of your life! May as well get high!"

That was all the convincing I needed. As Al rolled up the weed I dove head first into the blow. We only invited a hand full of people and in no time the small gathering was in full swing.

We smoked, drank, and snorted as we watched raunchy x-rated videos. The movies has us all hot and bothered when a knock on the door provided some relief.

"The entertainment is here," Al announced, rubbing his hands together greedily as he went to open the door.

A trio of trench coat clad women stormed in getting everyone's full attention.

"Which one of you tricks is getting married?" A thick light skin, green eyed beauty demanded.

All fingers pointed at me and she marched over. Without a word she knelt in front of me and began to blow me. The room was silent for a few moments except for the stripper's slurps.

"Y'all gone just watch dem or y'all tryna do something," a pretty dark stripper asked.

"Shit get busy," Al demanded.

"Ayo this my personal right here," DeSean announced producing a CD. "Put this in."

"Ok, D-lite! Yeah son the truth!" Al said accepting the selection.

When D-lite's 'Whose Pussy' came on, the other two girls disrobed and got busy.

Watching the sexy girls dance while getting head was too much. I held the strippers head in place and exploded in her mouth.

"Mmmm," she moaned greedily as she swallowed it down. "Next!"

She got up and the dark skin girl came and took her place. When she finished the next one came over and blew me too.

The sun rose around the time the party ended. We said our good-byes and headed in different directions. My friends to get some well needed sleep and me off to my wedding. Back at the condo I decided to take a ten minute power nap before heading out. The next thing I knew my dad was standing over me.

"Going to your wedding son?" Dad chuckled.

"Huh? My what?" I tried to make sense of his words.

"Come on son." He took me by the arm and guided me to the bathroom. I fought the urge to throw up and did fine until I brushed my teeth.

"Like father, like son," my father laughed as I threw up champagne and chicken wings from the night before. "I did the same thing on my wedding day."

My father left for a second and came back with a shot of cognac. "A little of the hair of the dog that bit you."

I didn't question my dad, just tossed it back. In seconds I felt better.

"Now hurry up. I'll be in the car," my father said as I finished dressing.

My mind flashed to the small amount of coke I left with. I reasoned that it too was 'hair from the dog that bit me' and quickly inhaled it.

When we reached the chapel, it was time to go to the altar and exchange vows.

"Glad you could make it," Prentice said through clenched teeth when she finished her march up the aisle.

"Me too," I chuckled, but she wasn't amused.

Our reception was a swank affair held at the Aquarium downtown. A carriage ride around the block completed the festivities and it was off to Hawaii for two weeks.

CHAPTER TWELVE

B ack in Atlanta we began our life and it was better than I could
have imagined. We lounged around for another week before it was
time to get down to business. For Prentice that meant beginning law
school. For me it meant my first day of work at the firm.

If there were any hard feelings about the boss' son coming straight
into a management position, I couldn't tell. I got along great with
everyone and made friends quickly.

One friend was Brian. He and I talked in the break room a few
times and then started chillin' together at lunch. I learned he was like
me, a recent graduate just entering the workforce.

He was also recently married, so we made plans to get our wives
together in hopes of it freeing us up to hang out sometime. Prentice
was the ideal wife. As eager as she was to excel and get her law degree,
she put us, the family first. Her course load revolved around me and
being able to take care of her home.

Being married freed her of all inhibitions and our sex life was
complete. I never even thought about other women. There was no
need. I got everything I needed at home.

Besides the social glass of wine at dinner I'd been clean and sober. I
did yearn to get high on a few occasions. I even dreamed about
smoking primos once or twice. A few times I contemplated on actually
smoking one but had no idea where to get the stuff. I wasn't going
anywhere near Mel again.

"What you studying so hard?" Prentice asked plopping, down on
my lap.

"You of course," I lied, pulling her closer.

"Oh yeah," she replied in between kisses, "what you thinking about me?"

"Trying to figure out what position to put you in," I replied with kisses of my own.

"Well mister," she said, removing her clothes," we will just have to try them all since you can't decide."

The next week Brian suggested over lunch that we hang out. I told him about my escapades in the strip clubs and he was dying to check one out.

"OK, here's the plan. You and your wife come over for dinner. Once they get to know each other Prentice will let me get out a little," I advised.

"Let?" Brian asked with a raised brow.

"Yeah, let!" I laughed. "You don't know Prentice.

~

B rian and his wife arrived with a bottle of wine and a cake for dessert. I'd never met his wife before but was in shock when I did.

"Will this is my wife, Angel." Angel...a perfect name for such an angelic looking woman. She stood about 5'6" and possessed a set of slanted eyes that betrayed her race.

"How are you?" I smiled, averting my eyes from hers only to get stuck on her breasts. I quickly turned away and called for Prentice to continue with the introductions. Over dinner the women discovered they were sorority sisters and made plans to get together.

Brian and I smiled at each other knowing our own play date was now confirmed. Still I couldn't take my eyes off Angel. I fell in love in an instant. She wasn't just pretty or fine. She was funny and personable with a laugh that sounded musical.

After the meal, Prentice gave Angel a tour of the condo while Brian and I slipped out onto the balcony.

"Say, you smoke?" Brian asked pulling a blunt from his pocket.

I shook my head no, but the word 'yes' came out of my mouth. Brian paused shrugged, then lit the weed. After a few tokes, he passed it, I took it, I smoked it, and I loved it. It felt so good to get a buzz—like an old friend had come home from a long journey.

Back at work we remarked how well the girls hit it off. I was tempted to ask him how a regular looking dude like him ended up with a woman as beautiful as Angel. That night after they left I made love to my wife with his wife on my mind.

One night our wives linked up for a sorority function and we hit a strip club. We smoked a nice blunt before we left out and Brian kept excusing himself to use the bathroom. Every time he'd come back sniffling and unconsciously rubbing his nose.

Once we got to the club we had more drinks and Brian resumed his disappearing act. After the third time, I knew what was going on and confronted him. "Set it out," I demanded knowingly.

"Huh? Set what out?" he asked unconvincingly.

"The blow B, set the blow out," I laughed.

"I'm saying though, I ain't know if you got down or not and ain't want to offend you," he said slipping me a glass vial.

It was one of those head shop bottles that had a built in scoop. I rushed into a bathroom stall and put three scoops in each nostril. I felt like I was home again.

Let's hit V.I.P.," I suggested when I returned. I felt like my old college self and it was time to live a little.

My face still held some weight and we were admitted into the ballers only V.I.P. section. As soon as I sat down a dancer flew over and plopped down onto my lap.

"Long time no see," Mel sang cheerfully. I heard you got married.

"I did," I said, trying to push her off my lap before my body reacted to her. Too late.

"Mmm I see you miss me though," she laughed, grinding her pussy that I know was wet, all up on me. It's been a while but I ain't forget a piece like that.

"Chill shawty." I tried again to push her up.

"You scared?" She grinded harder.

"Yeah, I'm scared you gonna make me bust in my pants," I said, looking over at Brian who was getting the same treatment from a dancer called Jewellz. I hit Jewellz a few times so I knew my friend was in trouble.

Mel and I chit chatted once I finally pried her off my lap. A few minutes later Brian is up and heading out the door.

I gotta get home, he says urgently over his shoulder to me.

I took Mel's new number and lied about calling her soon, then took off to catch up with my friend. He was already at the car when I got outside.

"What got into you," I inquired.

"That girl!" he said in amazement. "She made me cum in my pants!"

"Yeah, I should warned you about old Jewellz," I laughed. "Hope you saved something for your wife."

"Oh she in trouble when she get home," he laughed. "Plus I saved her a little blow, Angel a super freak when she get high!"

The thought of his beautiful wife getting high somehow turned me on.

CHAPTER THIRTEEN

A bout a month after the strip club visit, our firm sent Brian to Alabama to head up a project that was overdue. Since they were so far behind, they would work seven days a week for at least a month.

I came home from the gym one night to find Prentice and Angel laughing loudly in the den. The empty wine bottles and non-stop giggles explained it all.

"Hey baby, we were just talking about you!" Prentice chuckled and Angel cracked up.

"Okaaay?" I laughed before heading in to take a shower.

I decided to soak my knee and smoke a blunt. When I finally returned downstairs, my wife had passed out. After failed attempts to wake her, I picked her up and carried her to bed.

"You gonna come back and keep me company?" Angel asked sweetly.

"Sure," I said eagerly. I took Prentice to our room, changed her into her nightgown and made sure she was sound to sleep while thinking about the beautiful woman sitting in my den.

"We was 'posed to have a sleepover but Prentice fell asleep on me," Angel pouted.

The way she poked her lip out made me hard. They had gotten comfortable in shorts and Angel's thick legs had my full attention.

"Got some weed?" she asked, joining me on the sofa.

Instead of answering I leaned in and kissed her. It was a risky move, but I caught her looking at me as hard as I looked at her.

Angel pulled back and stared at me seriously. She looked to be in deep thought for a few seconds before nodding her head and removing her clothes.

The thought of my wife being so close only intensified the sex. Angel, slowly and quietly rode me until I came in her.

Afterwards, I ran in to check on my wife. I gave her a nudge that failed to wake her and then I hurried back to the den. This time I was on top and I gave Angel a thorough pounding until we came together. I again checked on Prentice.

We went on like that for hours. I woke up on the floor with Angel.

"Oh shit!" I exclaimed at our situation. I jumped up and hit the shower only a few seconds before Prentice walked into the bathroom.

"Hey baby, I'm sorry," Prentice sang, sticking her head into the shower.

"Oh you cool baby," I said, washing Angel off of me. The thought of Angel made me hard again.

"For me?" Prentice said, dropping her nightgown and climbing into the shower with me. I shrugged my shoulders and gave her the business too.

After the romp in the shower, Prentice went off to make breakfast for the three of us. Whenever I made her cum real good, she'd cook and sing. When I walked into the kitchen, both her and Angel were singing a duet as they cooked.

"Baby, I'm about to run," I said quickly, trying to avoid Angel's gaze.

"Honey," I'm making you breakfast, plus I need you to take Angel home," Prentice whined.

I started to complain and make up an excuse but when I looked at Angel she slid a finger in her mouth and pretended to give it head.

"No problem," I said, taking a seat at the table.

Angel and I rode in silence most of the way to her house.

"You feel bad about last night, huh?" Angel finally asked.

"Yeah, I guess, I mean I do," I said with mixed emotions.

"Me too," she replied with a wicked grin. "We ain't gonna do it no more."

She then reached over and removed my dick from my sweat pants and slid her lips around it. I was doing 35 miles an hour swerving to avoid cars. Finally, I pulled over and pulled Angel on top of me. She rode me right there on he side of 285 in broad daylight.

When Brian returned home I purposely avoided him. I really did feel bad about sexing his wife almost daily while he was away.

"Hey Willie, what's up?" We finally came face to face in the break room.

"Huh, oh cool," I stammered unsure of what to say.

"Angel told me you guys took good care of her while I was gone," he smiled.

"Um... no problem," I replied nervously.

"What's up Willie? What's wrong with you? You seem distracted."

What's up? What's up is...I've been sexing your wife since you been gone and I like that shit, I thought to myself. "Just got a lot on my mind, man. Sorry. Yeah, everything was cool while you were away. Our wives seem to be building a nice friendship."

"That's what Angel said. I'm glad since I may have to go away again. Let's plan for the four of us to do something soon."

"Okay, let's do that," I answered although I'm not eager to spend time with him, just his wife.

I felt so bad about sleeping with Angel and liking it the way I did that I stayed up under Prentice for weeks. She urged me to get out and do something but I just wanted to stay home...safe from temptations.

The phone range and I saw Brian's name on the caller ID. I'd still been ducking him because he wanted to go out and I really didn't want to hang out with him.

"Hey, that's Brian. Tell him I'm sleep," I said, handing Prentice the cordless phone.

"He sure is...I sure will...OK."

"Why you ain't tell him I was sleep?"

"He's up the street and said he's coming to pick you up. You need to get out. I have a ton of work to do." Prentice smiled.

When I got in the car with Brian, I still refused to go to the strip club. Instead I told him about Al's invitation to watch the fight at his house and we agreed to take him up on his offer. I hadn't hung out with Al in ages so we were both happy to see each other. I introduced him and Brian and they hit it off instantly.

We rolled up a few blunts and drank beers as the fights rolled on. When Brian excused himself to the bathroom, Al fished a package from his pocket.

"Your man get down?" he asked, showing me a nice size bag of coke.

I felt my mouth get watery and my stomach flutter at the sight of the drug.

"I said...do ya man get down?" Al repeated, alerting me that I hadn't answered him.

"Um yeah, we'll take a little," I said helplessly.

When Brian returned, we took turns snorting lines off the table as the fights raged on.

I felt a flurry of emotions as the drug coursed through my system.

"You fucking up," I warned myself. "I love it!" I admitted to myself.

The drugs obviously had the same effect on all three of us. We ended up going to the same strip club I vowed not to go to anymore. Al and Brian were having the time of their lives, while I was deep in thought, knowing I shouldn't have gone there. *Were the flood gates back open? Was this a one time thing? What now?*

"Looking for me?" Mel said, plopping down on my lap.

"Chill Shawty!" I snapped, pushing her off of me.

"Dang! What's wrong with you?" she asked as she hit the floor.

"My bad," I said, pulling her up and back on to my lap. "You trying to get me in trouble."

"Oh yeah, keeping forgetting youse married now," she teased.

"That's right! And I can't be coming home smelling like baby oil with glitter all over me," I laughed.

"Ayo son, ya boy wide open!" Al came over and announced. I looked up in time to see Brian enter a V.I.P. room with two dancers.

"Yeah Jewellz made that nigga bust in his boxers last time we came here." We laughed and Al made his way back over to his next lap dance.

Me and Mel spent the next hour or so just talking about old times. When Brian finished tricking, I gave Mel a hundred dollar bill.

"What's this for?" she asked, looking at the bill strangely.

"For your time. You coulda made twice that all the time you spent with me," I replied.

Boo, my time is always free for you," she said attempting to return the money. "Well at least come see me some time."

"I will. Promise," I lied.

CHAPTER FOURTEEN

With Prentice studying for exams, she pushed me out the house on a regular basis. I hung out with either Brian, Al or both.

Most nights we ended up in the V.I.P. room of some strip club. Temptation wore me down and I found myself at Mel's door.

I stood there at the door for a while, debating on whether or not to knock. Finally I decided to turn around and go home. As I descended the steps, a familiar face began to ascend.

"What up shawty," the young dealer who served us last time I was over there drawled.

"We was just waiting on you," I said, changing plans. I took care of him and headed back to Mel's door.

Mel was happy to see me standing on the other side of the door when she swung it open. She was expecting her delivery but instead she got me and her delivery. She and I got high for several hours between bouts of sex. When the time came for me to leave, I dreaded leaving both Mel and the remaining primo blunt. She made me promise to return and this time, I kept my promise. Often.

∼

My first wedding anniversary rolled around and Prentice pulled out all the stops. She rented an entire restaurant to accommodate our family and friends. Heart to Heart Band was hired to play their dead on renditions of all the latest hits.

Brian and Angel ended up at our table which made me highly

uncomfortable. I'd been avoiding Angel like the plague. When Brian refused to dance with her, Prentice ordered me to join her on the dance floor. I said "NO" so profoundly it made everyone take notice.

"OK, just one," I chuckled in an effort to play it off.

As soon as we neared the dance floor, the bank switched from an up tempo song to a slow one.

"Gotcha now," Angel laughed as she closed in for a slow drag. "Fucked up how you been playing me."

"We both agreed not to mess around no more," I reminded her.

"I see you changed your mind," she chuckled, slyly pressing her crotch against my stiffening manhood and backing away, careful not to draw attention to what was going on.

"You know Brian is going to Florida next week," she said seductively.

"I know, I'm sending him," I replied, staring directly in her slanted eyes.

Angel and I spent every night together. Her husband was right, she was a freak when she got high. She introduced me to anal sex once her period began, and like everything else in life, I got turned out on that as well.

When Brian returned from Florida his behavior had changed dramatically. It was almost like he left the real Brian in Miami and sent a clone.

Prentice told me Angel complained he hardly stayed home most nights. Mel explained it was because he was with Jewellz on a regular basis.

Dude was getting turned out. He was showing up late for work more often, and pulled a few no show Mondays. My father knew we had become friends and asked me to intervene.

When Prentice told me Angel said he moved out completely I decided it was time to talk to him. It took a couple of days to lock him down, but I finally got him out to lunch. We went to a local pool hall, ordered our food and grabbed an open pool table.

I noticed his appearance had changed. Nothing drastic, just not the same attention to detail he once showed.

We selected a sports bar so we could shoot a little pool over wings. After discussing local sports I finally got around to the matters at hand.

"You know you trippin' don't you?" I asked off handedly.

"Say what?" he inquired with his face twisted.

"I'm saying, you left your wife? For a stripper?" I questioned. "You ain't shaved, need a haircut. What's going on?"

"Hold up!" he demanded. "You asking me about my personal business? What I do off work ain't your business!"

"Ok, if it's like that, then you fucking up at work too!" I said with the sting of his words evident in mine. "You come in late; you pulled a couple no call no shows. If you wasn't my friend, you would've been fired!"

"Do what you gotta do!" he exclaimed before tossing the pool stick on the table and storming off.

I paid for the meal and headed back to the office. When I reached the parking garage, my cell phone rang, showing *Brian's house,* so I pulled into the first empty stall to take the call.

"Hello."

"Hey Will, this is Angel," she sighed wearily. "Just wanted to say goodbye."

"Goodbye? What's up? Where you going?" I asked.

"Back to Ohio," she said, fighting tears.

"Ohio! What's there?" I inquired.

"Home! Shit what's here? My husband left me for a damn stripper!" she sobbed.

As we spoke she told me how much money was missing from their account. She filed for divorce and froze their assets while there were some left.

Brian pulled into an empty stall catching my attention. We both had assigned spots one level up, so I watched to see what he was up to.

Whatever it was, it had his full attention. If he looked up we would have been eye to eye. I could hear Angel still talking but my focus was on her husband.

Brian put a glass pipe to his mouth and lit a lighter. His eyes grew big as saucers as he inhaled deeply. Strangely, I found myself inhaling along with him.

"Helloooo," Angel said frustrated at the fact I hadn't responded.

"My bad, you know what, I'm on the way over," I said, putting the car in gear. As I pulled out I honked the horn at Brian. I wanted him to know I saw him.

I called my secretary to let her know I wouldn't be back for the day. Instead of our outrageous sex romps, Angel and I took a walk through Piedmont Park.

I didn't tell her what I witnessed but did assure her she was doing the right thing. She needed a friend right then and I was there for her. We hugged tightly when it was time to depart, agreeing to link up when or if she came to town.

Brian didn't last much longer at the job. The final straw came when he didn't show up for a job in South Carolina. There was no need to fire him...he simply never came back.

I learned from Mel that he had began selling drugs to support his and Jewellz habits. Jewellz handled transactions at the club and sold to an undercover cop. She promptly set Brian up on a larger sale to save herself.

The four ounce sale got him ten years for trafficking. He vowed to kill Jewellz when he gets out.

CHAPTER FIFTEEN

That whole business of Brian unnerved me. I was shook up to the point again of staying home. No clubs, no Mel, and no more primos. Prentice noticed the change and inquired about it. Since admitting that I quit smoking crack blunts and sexing strippers wasn't a good look, I shrugged my shoulders.

Gradually our lives grew back together. She picked up on my sexual needs so it was no surprise when she announced we were pregnant.

I was ecstatic at the prospect of becoming a father. I doted over Prentice, catering to her every need. If she wanted a burger at two in the morning I went and got it.

When the big day came, it hardly seemed as if nine months had passed. Since the doctors scheduled a c-section, we knew exactly when our child would be born.

Angel flew in town the day before so she could see Prentice and be there for the birth of our baby. I felt a stirring in my loins just hearing her name. My wife cut off sex a month ago so I was. horny. I vowed not to cheat, but had a raging erection just thinking about Angel.

We got checked into the hospital with the camera rolling the whole time. They asked me to wait in the family room while they prepped Prentice for the surgery.

"Hey stranger," Angel sang when I entered the family room.

"Hey yourself," I said cheerfully but kept my distance. "So how are you? How have you been?"

"I'm good. Back in school, divorce final and good thing I froze the account when I did. You know that man spent ten thousand dollars in one month?"

"So, how is ole boy making out?" I asked, genuinely concerned.

"We write," she admitted. "No chance at getting back together but I don't hate him."

"Mr. Champion?" a nurse came out singing. "You can follow me."

Angel stood and gave me a hug before I left with the nurse. "Tell her I'm out here."

"I will."

A little while later I went out to the family room. When I stepped inside, I cleared my throat. Angel immediately looked up.

"There's a young lady that would like to make your acquaintance," he told her.

She and I made a beeline into the room.

"Hey sweetheart," I said softly. "Look who I found."

My wife handed me our daughter while they did the happy girl-friend hugs and shed their tears. After a few minutes Angel came around and took the baby.

We all turned when the door opened. "Congrats!" the delivery doctor said re-entering the room. "Well baby's fine but Mom's got some concerns. Your temperature is slightly elevated. We don't think it's anything serious but we want to watch you for 24-48 hours."

"Can my baby stay with me," Prentice asked.

"Oh of course. This is just precaution. Just a day or two tops," the doctor stressed.

"OK," she replied. "Angel you're staying at our house, no hotels."

"No, it's fine..."

"I will not hear of it, besides Willie needs company," Prentice demanded.

"Okay, okay. I'll stay." They hugged again.

Angel and I shot each other a split second glance that spoke volumes.

Still, I was committed to being committed. After driving Angel to the condo, I gave her a key and headed over to Al's.

He talked me into a blunt, which required a beer and led to snorting a few lines. He was right, it was just a celebration. I begged off going to a club and headed home.

On my way home, I called to see if Angel needed anything and to let her know I'd be there soon.

"Just walk in. Say goodnight. Go to bed," I mumbled to myself over and over as I walked up the front steps. My plans changed instantly when I turned the doorknob.

There was Angel naked on the sofa. She held one breast to her mouth and worked her clit with the other. Her timing was perfect—she came just as I walked in.

Since there was nothing to say, I went over and replaced her finger with my tongue. One deft maneuver later we were engaged in a vigorous sixty-nine. After making each other cum, I turned her over and gave it to her like I knew she'd been wanting it. We didn't sleep at all that night.

For the next 48 hours, Angel and I were either at the hospital or sexing each other at my house.

Prentice was happy to have received a clean bill of health and came home with our child. Angel stayed one more day, wished us well and went back to Ohio.

~

I ended up with a lot of free time since my wife was so busy with the baby. Al took advantage of my new spare time and talked me into hitting the clubs regularly.

We found ourselves in the V.I.P. room of our favorite club, sipping champagne, taking in hits of coke. I kept expecting Mel to plop down in my lap at any second but she never did.

I did see Jewellz and was shocked she was still working.

"Where your girl?" I asked curtly, hoping to avoid needless conversation.

Oh she don't work here no more," she said like she enjoyed it. "She falling off. Dancing at Crystal City on Bankhead."

"She aight?" I asked concerned about her dancing on Bankhead. I had never been on that side of town, but hear it's pretty rough over there.

"I don't know," Jewellz shrugged. "You want a dance?"

"Nah, I'm cool. How's Brian?" I said, hoping that would get rid of her and it did.

"Was that who I thought it was?" Al inquired as he returned from tricking off.

"Yeah that was her trifling ass," I spat. "Say what's up with Crystal City?"

"On Bankhead? That shit's a dump. Bitches got c-sections and tampon strings," he replied with a grimace.

I couldn't wrap my mind around Mel dancing in some dump. She was one of the finest in the city. She'd been featured in a couple rap songs and videos.

It was that curiosity that guided me towards Bankhead Highway after dropping Al back at home.

"Not so bad," I remarked aloud as I pulled into the parking lot of Crystal City. The area was indeed rough but the club appeared kinda nice. Club Chocolate catered to the ballplayers and rappers, while Crystal City appealed to the ballers and trappers.

My Lexus fit right in with the other nice cars in the lot. I set my alarm with a chirp and went inside.

I intended to hit the V.I.P. section but it appears one needs gold teeth for entry. Just as I opted for a seat at the bar I heard a familiar voice calling my name.

"Willie!" Mel sang before embracing me. "What are you doing here?"

"I came to see you," I said, accepting her tight hug.

"How you know I was here?" she asked.

"Jewellz," I replied

"That bitch!" she spat. "What else her lying ass had to say? That bitch be lying."

"Nothing, why what's going on?" I asked.

"Ain't shit going on. Hold up, I'ma get dressed and you can give me a ride," she said, taking off before I could respond.

I flirted with the idea of leaving, but that didn't feel right. The coke I had snorted with Al had worn off so I was a little hungry. I decided Mel and I would grab a bite then I was going home.

Mel came back in her street clothes looking like a teenager. Reminded me of when we met years ago when I lost my virginity to her. I hoped she didn't notice how hard I was when I stood.

Over breakfast she explained about her insurance lapse and the car wreck that claimed her vehicle. Perhaps that's what Jewellz meant by falling off.

When I got to her apartment on Glenwood Road, I left the car running with plans to leave.

"Aight shawty," I said, indicating I wasn't staying.

"Yeah right," Mel chuckled as she got out. "You better come on in here and get your dick sucked."

I told myself not to go as I opened my door, got out and followed her inside.

Make yourself at home, I'll be right back," Mel said.

She returned a few minutes later wrapped in a towel with wet hair. Without a word, she knelt in front of me and kept her promise.

I looked at the clock as she pleased me and shook my head. It was almost three, I should have been home. *Oh well, I'm hear now.* I leaned back, removed the towel from her head, grabbed the top of her head and led her motions. Mel cleaned me up once she finished and again I tried to leave.

"Aww baby at least stay and smoke one with me," she pleaded.

I debated with myself for two or three seconds before agreeing. The tightly rolled primo brought back too many memories. I knew I was fucking up, but it felt too good.

After smoking her dope, I felt it only right to lay some pipe. I dropped my pants, pulled her on top of me and she rode us to a mutual climax.

"Wanna smoke another one?" Mel asked excitedly as she cleaned our juices off of me.

"Umm...OK. Just one more," I agreed as I checked the time once again.

Mel frantically searched for another cigar or even a rolling paper but came up empty. I felt some kind of way about her desperation, but in truth felt the same.

"I got a shooter," she said solemnly.

My mind flashed to Brian smoking the glass pipe at work and his current situation. Taking all of that into consideration, I still nodded my head in agreement.

Mel produced an obviously well used straight shooter from under the sofa. I watched as she broke off a small piece of crack and loaded it in the pipe.

I was mesmerized watching her twist and turn the glass pipe under the flame of a lighter. I found myself inhaling with her as a steady stream of smoke raced the short distance.

She sank her beautiful naked body back into the sofa with a look of pure ecstasy on her face. Her eyes were closed and a pleasant smile adorned her face.

Mel handed me the pipe and broke off another rock from the cookie of crack. I felt like I was in trouble as I accepted it.

If I felt like I was when I took it, I knew I was when I hit it. The blast went from the pipe straight to my brain. Instant high! My whole soul was numb! I joined Mel against the sofa cushion and enjoyed the rush. Soon, I felt the effects waning and wanted another hit.

Mel obviously felt the same and fixed up a blast for herself. Once she finished, I followed. We continued like that until the cookie was depleted.

I glanced at the clock again and shook my head. It was 7:00 a.m. My mind scrambled for excuses when my cell phone vibrated. A glance at the caller ID told me I'd missed several calls. That wasn't surprising since my pants had been off for hours.

I was relieved to see Al's name instead of my wife's.

"Ay yo son where you at B?" Al asked urgently when I answered.

"Over here wit ole girl," I admitted sheepishly.

"Yo your wife been calling. I told her you was on the sofa drunk, then she said she was on the way so I told her you just left," he explained.

My phone beeped and *home* appeared on the display. I looked to Mel to make sure she wouldn't talk when my wife and life was on the line. She was too busy crawling on the floor looking for a contact, her earring or something she was mumbling about. Whatever it was would keep her occupied while I talked to Prentice.

"Hey baby," I said, straining my voice to fit Al's lie.

"Hey yourself mister," she said sympathetically. "Are you OK?

"Yeah, um...I...um...yeah...I'm fine, be home in a few," I stammered.

"Ok honey, I'll cook you something," she sang sweetly.

As I drove home, I thought of my conversation with Prentice. She was so nice even though it's the next morning and I'm not home yet. I couldn't have asked for a better woman and I just keep messing up.

When I got home, Prentice had a huge breakfast prepared for me. Before I sat down, my cell phone rang. It was Al checking to make sure everything was okay at home. After I assured him it was, I laid my phone on the table and sat down to eat with my daughter on my lap.

"Nadirah, let your daddy eat," Prentice said, reaching for our daughter who refused to go.

"She's OK," I said, sharing my food with my heart.

I realized at that moment just how undeserving of the two of them I was. It was then I again vowed to stay clean, stay home, and this time I meant it!

Prentice leaned down, wrapped her arms around me and our daughter and hugged the two of us.

"Oh, by the way," she said, "Angel called right before you got home. She said she'll be coming to visit soon and she told me to tell you hello. You know, I'm glad she and I became such good friends. With the divorce and all, she needs good friends like us. I think we should ask her to be Sadie's godmother. What do you think?"

Before I could respond, my cell phone rang. When I saw the name on the screen, I tried to grab it quickly. The screen read *Angel*.

Damn, did she see that? Why would Angel be calling me if she already called her? How do I explain this? My thoughts were racing, trying to figure out a logical explanation when I felt my wife move her hand away from me. When I turned my head to look at her, she had a gold hoop earring in her hand.

"Fuck is that?" I snapped defensively at the sight of Mel's earring. I knew exactly what it was since I was just sucking on it as she rode me just a few hours ago. I certainly wasn't mad but seeing the thing in my wife's hand scared the shit out of me. *Think, think!* I thought inwardly, desperately searching for a plausible explanation.

"Willie! Your mouth! And in front of Nadirah," she said, taking my daughter under protest.

"Where's the other one?" I asked, mock searching myself. "So much for a surprise."

"Oh you bought me earrings!" Prentice exclaimed happily and joined the futile search. "Well, it's the thought that counts. At least I have one," she conceded once the search came up empty.

My unanswered phone beeped, signaling that Angel had left a message. Curiosity was getting the best of me so I asked, "So when is Angel coming to town? I may hook her up with my man Al."

I had to fight against myself from getting hard at the mention of Angel's name.

"This weekend," Prentice replied, "for Nadirah's party. She's gonna stay here with us."

CHAPTER SIXTEEN

Boy time sure does fly. Whether you're having fun or not, time flies. It seems like only days ago that my daughter was born, but her first birthday is here already. She's walking and talking up a little storm. Of course I couldn't make out more than Momma or Daddy.

I was doing well with the not getting high part of my life. That's not to say I didn't think about it, cause I did...often.

I even dreamed about getting high. The shit be so vivid, I could hear the sizzle...even smell it! I would be taking hits off that pipe and holding it.

Prentice still pushes me out of the house, but I fight the temptations. I won't go near Al's house or a club. I just hit the 24-hour gym and catch pick up games or run some laps.

Even when my sexual urges get the best of me, I fight them as well. Prentice and I have a less than exciting sex life. I find myself masturbating to take up the slack. All that kinky stuff is out. She will hardly look at my dick let alone suck it!

Nadirah's birthday party was far more extravagant than any one year old needed. It was like she was the Princess of Monaco or some shit! They had pony rides, trampolines, piñatas and all kinds of stuff.

I drew the line at the parade of clowns they tried to hire. I hate fuckin' clowns. With two sets of well off grandparents, I didn't have to spend a dime or lift a finger.

"Babe," Prentice said, snapping me from my thoughts. "Angel's plane just landed. Can you go pick her up from the airport?"

"Yesss!" I said, jumping up from my chair.

"Dang Willie!" She frowned. "You that bored? Wanna get out of here that bad?"

"Bit much for me," I lied. I prayed she wouldn't look down and see how hard I was.

The whole drive to the airport I scolded myself. "Pick her up. Take her to the party. Do not touch!"

That sounded good until I saw her standing there on the sidewalk, patiently waiting to be picked up. The wind had caught her sundress and pressed it snug against her body. It made her appear almost naked in my mind.

"Hey Willie!" she sang as I pulled to a stop in front of her.

"Hey yourself," I shot back, getting out to grab her bag. Before I could reach down and get it, she hugged me.

"Mmm I missed you," she whispered grinding her crotch against me. "Do we have to go straight home?"

Now see, I was supposed to say yes. My daughter is having a grand celebration of her first year of life. Instead I drove to the top floor of the extended parking garage and found a spot in the corner.

I wasted no time in getting us in the back seat. Angel pulled her pretty panties to the side and I plunged inside of her, tongue first. There wasn't enough room for one of our famous sixty nines, so I ate her until she screamed.

She was still convulsing from the orgasm when I pushed inside of her. The excitement was too much for me. I came in seconds.

"I see you missed me too," she purred, stroking my back as I fought to breathe. The floodgates were open again. For some reason I wanted to get high!

Angel stayed at our condo for the weekend and I did my best to avoid her. That was despite her trying to seduce me every chance she got. Any time Prentice blinked, she winked. After the party was over and everyone had gone home, Prentice took a sleeping pill so she could get some much needed rest. Angel saw this as the perfect opportunity for she and I to go at it again. She even slipped into our open bedroom and sucked me off while Prentice slept at my side. I refused to follow her out into the den once she finished, so she climbed in the bed and rode me in super slow motion until we came. It was the best sex of my life.

Something about the possibility of getting caught only heightened the sex.

The next night I decided to get out and let them catch up. No, I left to get high. Sex and drugs went hand in hand for me since day one. I just got some incredible sex. Now I wanted to get high.

"Beers in the fridge!" Al said, stepping aside to let me in. "Grab me one too."

I returned with the green bottles and saw neat lines of cocaine adorning the table. I just dove right in, no sense fooling myself. That's why I was there.

Funny thing is, this all started again because I got some pussy. Then I wanted to get high, and now I want some pussy.

"Shit Shawty, let's hit the spot," I said, taking note of how much my speech patterns had changed. It was yet another subtle sign that I chose to ignore.

"Can't do!" Al said animatedly. "I got a stone cold freak on the way! Son you ever got your dick sucked until you pass out?"

"Um, well...no, I can't say that I have," I laughed.

"Ayo B, this bitch Charmaine got the best head in the world! Real talk son. Bitch gotta carry them paddles around—like clear—in case she stop a nigga's heart."

"Shit, if she a freak like that then I'ma chill here!" I said. "I want some defibrillator head!"

"This is a dolo move 'B', nigga might have to return the favor," Al laughed.

We snorted the rest of the coke off the table and I stood to leave. It was still relatively early so I contemplated what to do and where to go.

It didn't take me long to figure it out. Mel picked up on the first ring and invited me over.

"You just in time. Me and my girl was just about to fire one up," she said when I arrived. "Willie this Kenya, Kenya this Willie."

"Hey Kenya," I smiled at the thin, pretty, light complexioned girl seated on the sofa.

"Hey ya self. I heard a lot about you," she said wickedly.

"Good, I hope," I chuckled, taking a seat in the middle of the women.

"Mm hmp, good and big!" she laughed. Mel wasn't with the small talk. She lit a blunt and took a furious drag, then held it in as if her life depended on it.

The sizzle caught my attention and made me watch her smoke. Good thing I was seated in the middle because two tokes later I had the blunt in my hand. I took in the sweet, sickly aroma of the burning crack before taking a long overdue pull.

The cocaine infused smoke entered my lungs, then into my blood where it was distributed throughout my entire being. I actually felt it coursing through my body.

"Um Willie," Kenya smiled, "puff-puff-pass my nigga."

"Mmm hmph!" I agreed and complied, still holding the precious smoke inside my lungs. The blunt made a few more rounds before it was depleted.

"Well, that's the last of it," Mel announced sadly, poking out her bottom lip for emphasis.

"Call lil buddy up. I'll spring for the next go round," I offered. The plan was to stay over here for a while so I could stay out of Angel and thus out of trouble.

"That nigga done messed around and got himself locked up," Mel said disdainfully. "I can call Chubb. He got some fire."

"Wit his sweet self," Kenya laughed eyeing me again, then going into another coughing spell. The girl coughed like every five minutes or so.

It took about thirty minutes after Mel placed the call for the doorbell to ring. She peeped through the door's peephole to confirm he was who he said he was and pulled the door open.

In walked a squat, light skinned man who appeared to be in his mid to late thirties. He stood head to head with Mel, which put him at 5'5".

"Hey girl," he said sweetly and gave Mel a Hollywood hug.

"Hey Chubb," Mel sang, returning the hug with one foot bent into the air. "This Kenya, and my friend Will."

"Hey Kenya, hey Willie," he said studying me. "I know you!" He said with a 'where do I know you' from' frown on his face.

"You might, I get around," I replied dryly.

"Can we get a quarter of hard?" Mel sang sweetly.

"You sure can honey," Chubb sang back just as sweetly. Maybe even sweeter. "Two hundred."

Everyone looked to me, so I stood up to get some cash out of my pocket.

"Number 21," Chubb announced with a snap of his fingers, "point guard for Atlanta...Willie Champion!"

"That's me," I replied smiling from the recognition.

"Chile I'm an alumni! I used to love to watch you play! Just give me one fifty and here," he gushed going into his wallet and fishing out a card. "If you need *anything*... you holla, kay?"

"Um, yeah, OK," I said, feeling a bit uncomfortable at the feministic display. We made the exchange and he was on his way.

Kenya and I watched in total silence and anticipation as Mel rolled up a heavily laced primo. The silent room lit up with the crackling sound as she finally lit the blunt. I inhaled and held my breath along with Mel as she smoked.

Kenya went next, then finally me. Man that shit felt so good! *Mmm,*

I thought as the drug invaded my being. We all felt good. When Mel started kissing my neck I knew it was about to get better.

The second the blunt was finished Mel stuck her tongue in my mouth. As we made out, Kenya pulled my rock hard dick out and kissed it. I was in ecstasy when I slipped inside her mouth. After sucking me for a few minutes Kenya stood up and stripped.

"I'm finna ride this shit!" she announced, then mounted me. She slid down on top of me and began to rotate her hips in a circle.

"Damn girl," Mel chuckled as her friend got more into it. As she neared an orgasm she got more violent.

"Fuck!" Kenya yelled and began to come. I smiled watching her convulse as her pussy contracted around my dick.

"Next!" I laughed, gently pushing her off and pulling Mel on top. Mel tried to outdo her friend and rode me like a real horse.

A few minutes later she slumped off to the side after having an orgasm. I really wish I had a camcorder at that moment cause I gave both of them the business.

Kenya proved to be a bigger freak than Mel, and that's saying something. It wasn't until Kenya guided me into her ass that I came. I glanced at the clock and two hours had elapsed.

"I gotta push ladies," I said as Mel washed my dick. When she finished, I split the rock in half, pocketing mine and leaving the rest. "We gotta do this again. Soon!"

When I got home Prentice and Angel were still up talking. I peeked in the den and said goodnight before heading off to bed. I awoke the next morning with Nadirah playing in my face.

"Nadirah, let your father sleep," Prentice demanded in a whisper but it was too late.

"Hey baby," I said scooping my daughter up. I watched in horror as my wife picked up my shirt and the rock fell out of the pocket.

Prentice picked it up and stared at it curiously. To my relief she shrugged her shoulders and tossed it in the garbage can. I practically tossed my daughter aside to retrieve it as soon as Prentice walked out.

"I'm gonna run Angel to the airport. We need to finish talking. She thinking about moving back down," Prentice said.

I just grunted and rolled back over. I couldn't wait for them to leave so I could hit my rock. As soon as the front door closed I went to work. I had a raging piss hard on, so I wanted to relieve myself.

"The fuck?" I wondered at the strange yellow green puss oozing out my dick. That's when I felt it. It felt like I was literally pissing razor blades. I had been around enough to know I'd been burnt.

It took two days of pure agony for me to accept the fact that it wasn't going away. "Good thing my wife didn't want to fuck me." I chuckled and shook my head.

As fate would have it I saw Kenya at the same out of the way clinic I went to. She saw me as I walked in and averted her eyes. I then knew who I got it from.

I didn't plan on speaking to her anyway but I sat directly across from her just to make her feel uncomfortable. It was the least I could do.

In the bright light of the waiting room Kenya looked totally different. Different meaning bad. She appeared pale and sickly. Her coughing fits hit every few minutes, wracking her frail body.

Eventually it was me who felt uncomfortable and moved. No way would I have stuck my dick in her at all let alone raw, if I had seen how she really looked.

"Mr. Champion?" a pretty white nurse inquired.

"That's me," I said, flashing my best smile.

"Follow me," she instructed.

She reminded me of one of the cheerleaders at my school. I almost flirted until I remembered why I was there.

She led me to an exam room, told me to undress from the waist down and gave me one of those crazy gowns to put on that won't stay closed. Minutes later the doctor came in and immediately began asking me questions.

"Well, sounds like gonorrhea," the doctor announced after I explained my symptoms. He put on pair of sterile gloves and inserted a swab into my penis. "Probably should give you a blood test as well," he advised as he gave the cotton tipped swab an uncomfortable swirl in the head of my dick.

"I'm cool doc, a little clap is all I got," I said declining.

"These days we find two or three STDs at a time," he warned.

I'm good doc. Let me get a shot and be on my way," I demanded. The culture proved I did indeed have gonorrhea, at the very least. I got a shot in my ass along with the doctor's opinion of further tests, but again I declined. As soon as I got back in my car I dialed Mel's number.

"I just saw your girl Kenya," I said when she answered, "at the clinic."

"That don't surprise me, her nasty ass will fuck anything," Mel said. "Wait, what you doing at the clinic?"

"One of y'all nasty bitches burnt me," I said hotly.

"Oh so now I'm a bitch!" Mel shot back.

"Bitch you been a bitch! A nasty bitch at that..." That was all I could get out before she hung upon me.

CHAPTER SEVENTEEN

Over the next few months I hooked up with Chubb to exchange dope for dollars. Every time I went to his midtown apartment he had some half ass flirtatious shit to say. I guess he was trying me up, seeing if I would reply. I just ignored his gay ass.

"You so handsome...you work out?"

Fuck outa here! Taking his 'sweet' time to serve me so I would be over there longer.

One day while I was over there a beautiful, tall, woman came in. We had just completed our transaction and Chubb rushed me off.

As we passed one another, the woman and I exchanged knowing glances that spoke volumes. There was an unspoken mutual attraction that I couldn't just ignore. She was drop dead gorgeous and at least six feet tall. I had to have her.

When I left Chubb's apartment, I pulled out of eyesight and laid on the stallion. "Are you waiting for me?" she laughed as she pulled alongside my car.

"You were expecting me to weren't you?" I asked knowing the answer already.

"I would have been hurt if you didn't," she admitted. "I'm Cheryl."

"Willie," I replied never blinking.

"Well Willie, will you call me?" she said, extending a fancy business card.

"No doubt—if I don't, you call me," I replied, handing her my own card. "That's got my work, cell, fax and email. If you want I'll give you my mom's number too, or you can just yell my name loud and I'm on my way!"

"You're funny," she chuckled, "funny and cute!"

"Cute's for babies and puppies. I'm handsome."

"And modest," she laughed that musical laugh again. "Call me."

"I will," I assured her as she pulled away.

Cheryl and I flirted for weeks via text message and emails before we finally spoke. It took another week of marathon phone calls before we finally linked up.

Since I was smoking my little primos I was up most nights and so was Cheryl. We never talked about getting high, but considering we met at the dope man's spot it was pretty much a given.

It was a full month later that I saw her again. We met at a nice restaurant in Marietta that overlooked the river.

"Well, well, well...look what the cat dragged in," I joked when Cheryl arrived.

"Don't be talking about my cat," she laughed as she took her seat. The sexual banter lingered in the air for a second before the conversation continued. We chatted and drank more than we ate. I was soon following her to her house.

Cheryl lived in an upscale subdivision not far from the restaurant.

"I like!" I complimented as she led me through her house into a sunken den.

"There's a bottle of white in the mini. I'll be right back," Cheryl said, shooting me a seductive glance over her shoulder as she slinked off.

I opened the bottle and poured our glasses. When I sat down Cheryl returned. She traded the sexy business suit for more comfortable attire—T-shirt and panties—my favorite.

Our conversation picked up where we left off, still skirting the issue of why we were both at Chubbs. Finally I popped the question.

"So, how do you know our buddy Chubb?"

"Oh, same as you I suppose. Why were you there," she said diverting the question and redirecting back to me.

"I was copping," I said frankly.

"Hard or soft?" she asked.

"Hard," I replied. "I like to get high."

"Primo or pipe?" she said raising a brow.

"Primo, wish I had one now," I said honestly.

"Ta dah!" she laughed, producing a neatly rolled blunt like magic.

"Only problem is," I said seriously, then paused for added dramatics. "When I get high it takes me hours to cum!"

"You promise?" she asked eagerly.

I wasn't lying either. After we smoked the laced weed we went at it. I mean we fucked! Cheryl was an athlete in school so the sex was aggressive.

When she mounted me for a sixty-nine I almost balked, but her pussy was so pretty. It looked like lips puckering up for a kiss, so I kissed them. Then licked them, then sucked them, then she came. Then I came, then well...yeah!

CHAPTER EIGHTEEN

Cheryl ended up replacing Mel as my Friday night recreation. We occasionally stole moments during the week when it was possible. I didn't know what else she had going on in her life and didn't care. We got together when we could, got high and fucked.

That was my life for three years. I was maintaining my job, my family and my habit. I had my shit together, had a routine and then fucked that up.

"Mmm how bout that one right there?" Cheryl purred pointing to a thick dildo. She'd been talking about double penetration so we hit the head shop to pick up a helper.

"Nah, that's bigger than me. I'll get jealous," I laughed. "How about that one?"

"Dang man! Who's it going up in you or me?"

"Get the big one then," I answered quickly.

I was cool until we got to the counter. That's where they had their glass pipes displayed. My eyes shot to a perfect straight shooter. Instinctively I began slowly inhaling, almost hearing the sizzle.

"Um hello?" Cheryl laughed, breaking me from my trance.

"My bad," I apologized and paid for our new sex partner. "What time do you guys close?"

"Twelve," the clerk said stoically as he rang us up.

The sex, as incredible as it was, could not keep my focus. Even as the dildo and I traded places from Cheryl's vagina and anus, I still could see, taste and feel that blast from that pipe years ago with Mel.

By the time I finally satisfied that amazon it was almost 1:00 am. I felt mixed emotions about missing the head shop before it closed. On one hand, yeah I was gonna buy that straight shooter; then on the other hand, I was relieved that I dodged a bullet...for now.

When I got home, I showered and slipped in bed with my wife. That night and every night after, I dreamed about that damn pipe. Night after night, tossing and turning, until one day I bought it.

Still I didn't use it. I would sit it on the table and stare at it while I smoked my primos—the way men would stare at a porno picture and masturbate. Shit would have been funny if it wasn't so sad.

It finally caught up with my ass too. Prentice and Nadirah went to Alabama with her parents and left me alone in the condo. I got with Chubb and bought a whole ounce. I started out still tricking myself, watching the shooter while I smoked.

"Just a light one," I reasoned breaking a small piece of my cookie of crack. "Just a corner...a little blast," I said, making it seem fair.

"Great day in the morning! Good googly, moogly, shut my mouth!" All those exhortations and more flooded my mind as soon as that first hit hit my brain!

I had two days alone and I sat my ass there almost the whole time smoking. I barely ate, slept, showered or anything...just got high and jacked off. I don't know why but the shit made me horny, although I didn't want company. I even ignored Cheryl's constant calls.

By the time my family came home, I was frazzled! Dirty, unshaven, hungry, just looking crazy. For the next few days I was a beast. I'm talking major attitude. It wasn't until I was able to get high again that weekend, that I understood what was wrong with me. I needed a hit. In my befogged mind I was able to reason that if I smoked everyday it would keep me balanced. No more ups and downs. Just ups.

The result of that was more erratic behavior. I was late for work, missed days...just tripping, but like any other addict will tell you, it takes a major event to wake you up. Something has to force your hand.

"Baby, I'm going shopping with mother for Nadirah's birthday, so she's staying home with you," Prentice ordered as she prepared to leave.

I just granted a response. I really wanted to be left alone so I could get high. I made up my mind to stick Nadirah in front of the TV with a DVD and do me.

That's exactly what I did too, but kids will be kids. As soon as I got me a good blast she came knocking on the door.

"Daddy can I have some juice?" she yelled through my locked door.

"Go 'head!" I snapped, pissed at having to exhale before I ingested all the hit had to offer.

"I need you to get it," she whined with her little fussy self, just like her damn momma.

"You can get it yourself!" I shot back, assuming she meant a juice box.

Knowing that her mother wouldn't allow it, she decided to go for it since I made her get it on her own.

Nadirah pulled the bottle out of the fridge with no problem, then climbed on the counter to retrieve a glass from the cupboard. That part went well. It wasn't until she tried to descend with the glass that disaster struck.

My daughter lost her balance and tumbled to the floor, glass first. The heavy glass shattered and one of the pieces with a point the size of a blade, punctured her leg as she landed on top of it.

I don't really recall if I actually heard her scream of just felt it. Still I held that hit for all it was worth. When I went to investigate I almost fainted.

There was my precious child laying in a pool of blood with more blood squirting from the ruptured artery with every beat of her heart. I grabbed a dish towel and used it to apply pressure. Since she was losing so much blood I knew I didn't have time for an ambulance.

I rushed her down to my car and drove her myself with her lying on my lap so I could keep pressure on the wound. The dwindling amount of the squirting blood meant she was running out of the precious fluid.

After we arrived my vein was quickly tapped to replenish what she'd lost. We lay side by side in the emergency room as she received the transfusion.

"It's a good thing you guys share the same blood type," a nurse said patting my arm.

"Hell she can have it all," I replied sincerely.

I called Prentice and let her know what happened. She was in the room seemingly seconds after we hung up.

Oh was she hot! "So what exactly were you doing when our daughter's leg got amputated?" she growled.

"Amputated? It's not bad enough? Must you really exaggerate the issue?" I shot back. I already felt bad enough about the accident.

She stormed away and waited by Nadirah's side until they finished her care. Hours later we all left together, traveling silently back to the condo. I left my blood filled car and drove Prentice's car.

When we got home, Prentice carried our daughter, refusing to hand her over to me. Once inside I went straight to the kitchen to clean up the mess. No way did my wife need to see that. It looked like a massacre had taken place in there.

I just started mopping when Prentice started screaming my name.

"Willieeeee!" she yelled nonstop until I came running. I expected her to be in our daughter's bedroom but she wasn't. "Williee!"

"What?" I snapped, following her voice into our bathroom.

"What is this?" she demanded holding my pipe and bag of dope in the air. "Is this why you almost killed our daughter?"

I was speechless. What could I say anyway? I was busted. She was yelling and screaming but honestly, I didn't hear a word of it. I was too busy watching my dope. When she turned towards the toilet I sprang into action.

"Fuck you think you doing?" I yelled as I wrestled my crack and pipe away. She made a move to take it back and I shoved her down. Prentice stared up at me with a look of disbelief and shock pasted on her face.

Not knowing what else to do, I ran out of the condo. I had to protect my rocks...keep them safe. Since my car was still at the hospital I took my wife's.

Out of instinct, more than anything, I found myself in front of Mel's apartment. It had been years since I'd last been there but here I was. After a short debate with myself I got out and headed to the door.

An older lady answered and said she didn't know anyone named Mel and that she'd lived there for a couple of years.

I headed back up Glenwood then pulled into a shabby motel. I had to swerve to miss a crack head that staggered through the parking lot. I frowned at her trying to reconcile her face. She looked just like Mel, but it couldn't be. Mel was a stallion. This monster couldn't be her. "No way," I said. When I got out to look, she had already been whisked away by some trick.

The room stank like cigarettes but was in much better shape inside than I expected. I immediately fixed myself a blast. After all, first things first! Spent all day in the hospital, gave blood, now it's time for me. Some me time!

The only time I ventured out was for fresh lighters and beer. Every time I get high I get antsy...have to move. I usually wanna fuck something.

On my third excursion into the streets I ran into a cute little smoker. I knew she smoked cuz she just left the room of the renegades who were selling out of the motel.

"Where you headed?" I asked her as she passed by on the motel balcony.

"To the park, to smoke me one," she replied.

I guessed her age at late teens at best and was turned on.

"I got a room," I offered, "come hang out."

"I don't have to do anything?" she asked fearfully.

"Nothing you don't want to." I smiled. "Just need a smoking buddy."

She agreed and I led the way. After we got high, I fucked her like the world was about to end. Like the only way to save the planet was to fuck the shit out of her, so I did.

I left her in the room without even catching her name but left my business card. I rocked her fine lil ass to sleep so good she was snoring and drooling when I eased out. If I didn't pull the covers over her fine lil ass I would have never gotten out of there!

CHAPTER NINETEEN

It was early afternoon the day after Nadirah's accident when I finally made it home. I had been rehearsing what I would say the whole drive, but to my relief the condo was empty when I arrived.

The first thing I did was check the closets to see if Prentice had moved out. All her clothes and shoes were still there so I assumed she hadn't.

My cell phone was right on the table where I left it. It had so many missed calls, texts and voice messages that I just turned it off. I built up enough courage to pick up the cordless and call my wife.

"I see you made it home," she said so calmly it scared me. "As you can imagine we need to speak with you. Can you stay there until we get there?"

"Yes," I replied, "I'm not going anywhere."

It had been 24 hours since I had eaten. Now that I was thoroughly sober I was starving. I microwaved some leftovers and inhaled them. A serious case of 'nigga-it is' crept in and I couldn't keep my eyes open. It was all I could do to make it to bed.

"Son!" the faraway voice called, then repeated. "Son, wake up. I felt a firm shake and opened my eyes. There was my dad standing over me, with my mom close behind.

"Mom? Dad?" I asked confused by their presence. "What are you guys doing here?"

"We're here to speak with you son," my dad said gently.

"It's an intervention!" my mother said harshly. "Now get yourself together and meet us in the living room."

I brushed my teeth, washed my face, and peed thick, rancid, almost brown urine. Then headed to face the music.

My parents and wife sat stoically in the room awaiting my appearance. As embarrassed as I was, I was relieved that my in-laws weren't there.

My mom held no punches. She straight let me have it. She blasted me for twenty minutes about how disappointed she was in me—said she would have smothered me as a baby if she'd known I was gonna turn out like that.

Dad went next and coddled me as usual. He offered excuses for me that I didn't even think of. To him it started at my injury.

Finally my loving wife gave a tearful plea for me to get help. Afterwards she got up and walked into the bedroom.

It was my turn to talk, and I gave a little song and dance that my mother twisted her lips at. I always forget that she is from the hood herself.

"Son we enrolled you in a ninety day rehab center," my dad began before being cut off by my mother.

"You're going! No more excuses! No more bullshit! You're going!" she demanded.

On cue, Prentice came out with a tote bag packed with things I would need for my stay. I had no intention on going but accepted my fate.

"For better or worse," Prentice said with a forced pain filled smile, as she took my hand.

The four of us rode in silence to the center. It was in the middle of a large wooded area to keep us in I guess. I could imagine a junky wandering around in the woods trying to escape.

The thought made me chuckle but my mother shot me a glance that killed it. I looked at my dad just in time to see him knock away a tear. It was the first time I'd ever seen him cry.

"I'm good, you guys go home," I insisted once we parked. I hopped out and headed in without turning back to wave goodbye. I didn't want them to see my tears.

"Yes, can I help you?" An attractive older lady at the front desk asked with a welcoming smile.

"Um yeah, my name is um William Champion. I'm here to get help with my...I have a um...drug problem.

"We've been expecting you, Mr. Champion. You're in the right place," she said triumphantly.

The first couple of days were the worst. I almost tried those woods a couple of times. The only thing that kept me there was a gorgeous white girl I kept seeing.

Because of the busy schedules, I only saw her in passing and didn't get a chance to speak with her until one night I followed her into one of those meetings.

The structures during the day were mandatory but the group support meetings at night were not. I had no desire to sit there and listen to the *Chronicles of a Junky* as I called it, and I damn sure wasn't about to go up there and tell them my business.

Besides, I was nothing like them. I wasn't a junky. I just like to get high is all. Yeah my shit got a little out of hand, but I'm cool. I got this.

Just as I slipped into a chair in the rear, the lovely blonde haired, blue eyed girl began to speak.

"Hello, my name is Amanda," she began, then paused for all in attendance to say, "Hi Amanda."

"Well I'm here for the same as most of you guys. Drugs." She recounted how she began smoking weed at 12, her mom's pills by 13 and meth by 15.

She told the group how she milked her parents for all she could before they closed the tap, then began to steal items out of the house to sell for drugs. The statement made my mind flash to my own parents home. A person could get high for years off all the valuables they owned.

"Once that got me kicked out, I traded sexual favors for drugs," she said matter of factly. "I was passed around like a whore. I sucked so many cocks in one day it felt like my jaw was broken."

I didn't hear one word she said after that. I was rock hard at the thought. I might not be able to get high for ninety days but I'm gonna fuck something. When the session ended I waited for Amanda to come out.

"Hi, I'm Willie," I said with my best smile to go along with my outstretched hand.

"Well hello Willie," she said flirtatiously, holding my hand softly, "I'm Amanda."

"I heard what you said in there. It made me...um...well."

"Horny!" Amanda laughed, still holding my hand.

"That too," I admitted as the eye contact intensified.

"Yeah I told my therapist that story and he fucked me right there on that sofa," she laughed again.

"Where can I fuck you?" I said pulling her to me.

"We can go to my room," she suggested before leading the way. "My parents sprung for a private room." Once we arrived I was in her mouth in seconds.

She obviously knew that trick that snakes can do and unhooked her jaws cause she had my entire dick in her mouth, and I have decent size dick.

I missed college watching the pretty white girl blowing me. She didn't even budge when I began to cum. Instead she moaned and milked me dry.

"My turn?" She asked so sweetly I had to do it. I ate that pretty pink pussy until she begged for the dick. I gave it to her too.

Boy did I give it to her! I folded her little ass in half and tried to push inside her kidneys. We spent the rest of the program sexing every chance we got.

At night I spent hours on the phone with my wife. It took some doing but she finally forgave me. We agreed to give our lives a fresh start.

When I got home Prentice and I dropped Nadirah with her parents and we went on a cruise, a long overdue vacation. A week of sun and sex before returning to our lives.

CHAPTER TWENTY

When Prentice passed the bar she began working at a prestigious law firm downtown. At the same time I excelled at work. Life was good again.

I was back at the gym on Friday night—for real this time. My game was back too. One night I caught one off the rim and dunked.

"That's my daddy!" Nadirah yelled from the sidelines alerting me to their presence. I called time and ran over to the sidelines to my family.

"Checking up on me?" I asked when I approached.

"No, Yes," Prentice laughed. "Actually I took Nadirah to the E.R. she keeps coughing. *Then* we came to check on you."

"How's my baby?" I cooed, trying to pick her up.

"Eww daddy! You're wet!" Nadirah complained trying to get away from me.

"Come on champ!" One of my teammates yelled to get me back on the floor.

"Y'all go 'head. I'm 'bout to push!" I yelled back.

"Oh you don't have to quit your game!" Prentice said.

"I know I don't *have* to, I *want* to," I said leading my family away.

Nadirah seemed to be sick all the time—fevers, flu and coughing spells became the norm. She was always tired and lethargic. Doctors weren't telling us much then, just treating her for the usual childhood ailments.

"Go!" Prentice demanded one night. "You have to go back out into the world. You'll be fine. Go."

She was right. I did need to get out. I called Al and told him I was coming over. No drugs, no sex, just hang out with my buddy.

OK, now I did hit the blunt and drink a beer while I was there. That's OK cuz my problem was coke. He had some too, but I didn't touch it. I won't lie, my mouth was watering watching him snort those perfect white lines off the glass table.

When he suggested hitting Club Chocolate I quickly accepted. The last time we were there a pretty little black girl masturbated on stage. That shit was crazy.

We settled in the V.I.P. and it felt like old times...just like old times. Jewellz brought her nasty ass to the table. "Hey Willie. Heard about ya gurl?" she sang, happy to impart some gossip. "She dead!"

"Who dead?" I asked not really interested in her reply.

"Mel. Mel dead," she said still smiling as she delivered what should be bad news. "She had that pack! That monster!"

"AIDS? Mel had AIDS?" I asked, remembering the sorry shell of Mel I saw chasing cars. I was shook up. I was so shook up I felt like getting high, so I dropped Al off and headed to Chubb's house.

"Cheryl been trying to reach you mister," Chubb said sounding almost jealous. "Said you changed your number and don't call no more."

"Tell her I said hey," I said evenly.

"You heard Mel dead, AIDS," he said devoid of any remorse. I just grunted a reply. As bad as I felt about Mel, it bothered me even more how casual everyone was about it.

"You been working out? You look buff!" Chubb said emphatically. I just ignored him, again.

After leaving Chubb's house I rolled me up a nice primo and blazed it as I drove home, slowly. You already know I was high as a kite and horny as hell when I got there.

"Will you stop!" Prentice demanded as I tried to seduce her away from her laptop. I was far too excited for romance. I just rubbed my erection against her neck.

"Come on baby, five minutes," I said practically begging.

"I have far too much work to do," she said curtly. "Take a cold shower!"

"I think I'll take a drive instead," I said feeling wounded.

"Great! The fresh air will do you some good!" she spat at my departing back.

I reached my destination and pulled out my cell phone to announce my presence.

"Willie?" Cheryl asked at the sound of my voice. "Long time no hear from. What's going on?"

"I'm outside. I'm high and I'm horny," I replied.

"Well I hope you brought more than just your dick! Come on in," she laughed.

I went inside and gave her all I had to offer, coke and dick. That jump started our usual Friday night get high freak sessions all over again.

Only problem was that with my smoking again every day, I was horny every day. Prentice had virtually closed up the pussy shop and Friday was a long time from Friday.

A surprise call on a lonely Tuesday night came to my rescue. I was in the den twiddling my thumbs trying not to go over to Chubb's to cop. I really wanted to fall back a little. I saw I was slipping.

"Hello?" I questioned at the unfamiliar number in my phone.

"Hey mista, this is Denise. Member me?" she asked eagerly.

"Denise? From where?" I said wracking my brain to place the name.

"Um a couple months ago; in Decatur at the hotel?"

We did it. You gave me your card," she said jogging my memory.

As a matter of fact, my body remembered her as well, and I got hard instantly.

"Where you at? I'm coming to get you!" I said standing to leave. She gave me her whereabouts and I tore off to meet her. I was in such a hurry I didn't even bother to tell Prentice I was leaving. Probably wouldn't have noticed anyway.

I called Chubb en route and had him fix me up an ounce. Denise was at a pay phone just where she said she would be. It was across the street from the motel we had our romp months earlier.

Still, I was I the mood for something a little more upscale. I called ahead and got us a room at the Plaza. Denise was in trouble tonight!

"What's in the bag?" I inquired about the dingy knapsack at her feet.

"Everything," she replied with a humorless chuckle. "My momma put me out."

We rode in silence the rest of the way downtown. As I drove I contemplated how I could help her. I decided I could help her and myself at the same time.

"Don't worry I got you," I announced triumphantly.

"I can stay with you?" she asked reminding me of my daughter.

"Nah, my wife wouldn't go for that. I got something better in store," I said patting her firm thigh.

Denise complained she was hungry so I let her order whatever she wanted from room service. While she devoured her food, I took me a few pulls off a primo. Once she finished I thrust the blunt at her, eager to her high. Once the blunt was consumed I was ready to get down!

I got my period," she whined when I began to undress her.

"Fuck!" I spat, thoroughly disappointed. I resolved to settle for some head, but I really wanted to fuck her fine little ass.

"I don't do that," she whined again when I shoved my dick in her face.

"Look!" I demanded forcefully, "I'm about to get you a place to stay. Take care of you. You will do what I tell you to do!"

Reluctantly she opened her mouth and I pushed inside. She had officially become my sex slave. The head wasn't good, but I knew I could work with her. I stripped her down to her panties and put my erection between her large hard breasts.

I'm long enough to titty fuck and still have some dick in her mouth. When I finally came, I grabbed her head and forced her to take and swallow every drop.

Denise stayed in the hotel with strict instructions not to leave or call anyone. A few days later I found her a nice one bedroom apartment minutes from my condo. I took her to the local super center and bought her clothes and everything she could possibly need—TV, DVD, furniture, pots and pans—everything. My sex slave was set. I stocked the fridge and cupboards as well.

"Thank you so much," Denise sang as we sat on the just delivered sofa.

"You know how I like to be thanked," I said and leaned back.

Denise smiled broadly as she pulled my dick out. She put me in her mouth and thanked me thoroughly. I had it made! Of course with a young moldable, flexible, willing and able sex slave minutes from home, Cheryl was history. I neither took her calls or returned her messages.

CHAPTER TWENTY-ONE

W hen my one year graduation from rehab rolled around Prentice made a big deal of it. She was so proud and gushed about it all day. The shit just made me want a blast.

Really it was her fault, cause I was cool with my little primos but all that pipe talk wore me down. The next thing you know I was in the head shop picking out a straight shooter.

Denise had a look on her face that was a cross between horror and excitement when I pulled that shooter out for the first time. Only this time I didn't play with it. I put a rock on that bad boy and got to it.

I took a nice blast and fixed one up for Denise. She looked like she wanted to decline but I pretty much forced it on her like everything else. Last time she had her period I forced my way into her ass.

She didn't want to do it, but she didn't have a choice. Denise was the slave and I was her master. She took the pipe and sucked on it as I held the flame to it.

Of course being back on the pipe required a lot more of my time. I had to blow days off from work on occasion just to keep up. It was during one of these excursions that I received a frantic call from my wife.

"Willie? Where are you? I called your job and they said they don't know where you are! Where are you?" she rattled desperately.

"What do you want?" I said nonchalantly. I'm trying to get high and she stressing me.

"Nadirah collapsed at school! They took her to Children's Hospital," she said urgently.

"So what you want me to do?" I asked dryly, eager to get back to my pipe.

"What?" I want you to meet me at the hospital!" She screamed at the top of her lungs.

"Fuck! Aight, I'm coming," I said halfheartedly. "Still don't know what you need me for, I ain't no doctor!"

When I arrived I gave my name to two grim faced nurses, who frowned upon hearing it. They directed me to the room where my wife and child were. Prentice shot me a cold glance when I walked in then turned back to Nadirah.

"They don't have a clue what's wrong with her," Prentice lamented. "She still didn't wake up!"

"All these machines and shit and nobody know nothing!" Prentice frowned at me more because of my bad grammar than the outburst.

It was several hours before the doctor came back with news. Prentice and I sat by our child consumed in our own silent thoughts. I was sitting there hoping Denise didn't smoke the rest of my shit.

"Well," the doctor began, "I've run the test three times to confirm the results."

"OK, and?" I snapped. "Get on with it!"

Mr. and Mrs. Champion your daughter has several life threatening infections, all caused by and exacerbated by full blown AIDS. Your daughters T-cell...

"Excuse me? I'm sorry, did you say my child has AIDS," Prentice said aggressively. I held her shoulders to prevent her from approaching the already nervous doctor.

"Yeah, that can't be right! How the fuck a six year old gonna catch AIDS?" I demanded.

"Well I reviewed her records from birth. We have also examined and ruled out sexual abuse so..." the doctor paused

"So what? How the fuck my daughter get AIDS?" I yelled. Now it was Prentice's turn to hold me back.

"From you Mr. Champion. From the blood transfusion you gave her when she injured her leg," he said, sucking all the air out of the room.

Prentice released her hold and stepped back to look at me.

"I ain't got no fucking AIDS," I chuckled. "No way!"

"I'm afraid there is no other explanation. Of course we need to test you and begin your treatment," he said.

"What about my daughter? How will she be treated?" Prentice pleaded.

"Ma'am, your daughter is terminally ill. She will not recover. We'll also need to test you as well. If you have been engaging in marital relations, chances are extremely high that you're infected as well," the doctor said stoically.

"You fucking bastard," Prentice said just above a whisper. "You low life bastard," Prentice balled up her little fist and attacked.

"You killed us, you killed us!" She yelled as she punched my chest and face. I didn't even budge. Honestly it felt good. I'd been so numb from the drugs, I hardly felt anything for months.

When I got back to my little apartment Denise, was pulling on the pipe.

"Bitch I know you ain't sitting here smoking all my shit," I yelled.

"Just a little," she said apologetically and handed the shooter to me. I took it with one hand and delivered a thunderous slap with the other. Denise crumbled and cowered on the floor.

I broke a larger than normal, larger than necessary, larger than healthy piece off and loaded it on my pipe. After finally blowing that long needed hit out, I turned my attention back to Denise.

"How many times I gotta tell you to stay out my shit?" I demanded. The poor girl was stuck on how to answer the senseless question.

"You think it's a game huh? I'm a fucking joke huh? I said standing over her. When she opened her mouth to speak I slapped whatever she was trying to say across the room.

Denise screamed as she crawled away. A swift kick to her midsection flipped her over with a grunt. She was scooting away on her ass when I caught her.

"Turn your nasty ass over," I said flipping her back onto her stomach. I yanked the skimpy shorts that I made her wear off and snatched away her panties.

I was in a rage and it felt good. My dick was harder than ever when I began to anally rape her. All Denise could do was scream as I ripped into her.

When I finally came it was as if all the rage skeeted out of me with the semen. I slumped over, spent and calm.

"I'm sorry Willie. Whatever I did I won't do again," Denise promised. I rolled off to the side, allowing her to get free.

Instead of running out of the apartment to safety or screaming for help, she retrieved a hot soapy washcloth and cleaned the semen and feces from me.

"I'm sorry," I offered contritely as she washed me. She nodded acceptance and continued.

A pounding at the apartment door broke up our reconciliation. "Who the fuck is this?" I demanded standing up.

"Who!" I barked at the closed door.

"Atlanta Police!" came the stern reply.

Denise sprang into action and removed the drugs and paraphernalia from view.

"Yes, is there a problem officer?" I said like my old self.

"We got a couple 911 calls about a lady screaming?" the officer said peering into the living room.

"Well officer," I chuckled, stepping from my position behind the door so he could see I was clad only in my underwear. "My girlfriend and I can get quite audible at times."

"That's fine sir, can you please ask her to come out. Once I verify she is unharmed I can be on my way," he offered.

"Denise, honey?" I called sweetly to the rear of the apartment, "can you pop in for a second?"

"I'm not dressed," she wisely called back from just out of sight.

"Ma'am I can't leave until I can see you," the cop boomed back.

Denise walked out and the first thing we both saw was the huge lump over her eye.

"Turn around and place your hands behind your back," the officer demanded removing his cuffs.

"You arresting me?" I asked foolishly as the cuffs clamped down on my wrist.

"Yes, for domestic violence," he replied. "Ma'am you will need to come down and make a statement."

"A statement for what? He ain't touch me!" she yelled protectively.

"No matter, based on your bruises I have probable cause," he said through an invisible smile.

I was offered a phone call as part of the intake process at the jail but declined. After all who would I call?

Dad, I beat my girlfriend up cause Nadirah got AIDS? Imagine that.

My bail was set at $10,000.00 but it wouldn't have made a difference if it was ten bucks...I wasn't going anywhere.

I embraced the long awaited sleep. I slept for the first full day without even getting up to eat. Over the next two weeks the only thing I did get up for was to eat the slop they offered three times a day. No shower, no shave, no nothing.

"William Champion?" a guard said loudly as he stood over me. "You must not want to leave. We been calling you for twenty minutes! Pack it up. Your bail's been paid."

I dressed slowly wondering who paid my bail. I hadn't called anyone. My question was answered when I walked into the lobby and saw my dad.

"Dad?" I asked at his presence.

"I'm here son," he said embracing me. I knew I smelled badly, but none the less he held me tightly.

"Son, the funeral is tomorrow," my father whispered as we merged into midday traffic.

"Whose?" I asked genuinely unaware of what he meant. "Who died?"

He looked at me with a look of utter confusion before he spoke. "Nadirah. Your daughter. She passed away on Monday."

"Dad I ain't even sick," I begged." "Look at me! I'm as healthy as a horse! She did not get it from me. Maybe her mother, or from the hospital!"

"I know son, I know," he said patting my hand to comfort me.

"I can't go in there," I pleaded, seeing Prentice's car in its parking space.

"You have to son," my father said with authority. Your wife is the one who found you. She wants to talk to you. She needs you."

"Prentice!" I called out as I walked into the condo. "Prentice!" I called out going from room to room. I was actually relieved not to find her home.

At least I would have a chance to shower and shave before I spoke with my wife. I saw the Valium bottle on the counter and went for it. It was empty, though dated two days ago. I was puzzled about how fifty pills could be gone in two days time.

That is until I pulled back the shower curtains. There was Prentice submerged in the bloody water. Her wrists were sliced open and she stared back with dead eyes.

I slowly slid down the wall and wept. I now had to bury both my wife and daughter. I killed them both.

CHAPTER TWENTY-TWO

I sat alone at what had to be the saddest funeral in human history. As soon as mourners saw that tiny pink casket they lost it. Wails could be heard all over the funeral parlor. More than one overwhelmed woman had to be helped out of the room when it got too much for them.

My mother refused to even look at me. My father nodded at me but stayed by his wife. Prentice's dad stared at me with pure hate in his eyes.

The preacher stirred up more emotions with his trouble-making ass. Talking about lives cut short and bullshit. Fuck him. Since no one wanted me to ride with them, I followed the funeral procession alone in my own car.

Somewhere along the way I pulled off. Nobody wanted me around so I left. I went home and started drinking. I was good and drunk when someone began pounding on my door.

I pulled the door open without checking and paid for it immediately. As soon as the door opened I was met by a barrage of punches and kicks.

It took a second before I could see through the blows to figure out who was the bearer of the beat down. Once I recognized the assailant I lowered my hands and took the punishment.

Even when he pointed a pistol in my face I didn't budge. I braced myself for impact, eager to join my family.

"You're not even worth a bullet! I hope you rot in hell!" Prentice's father spat before literally spitting in my face. He lowered the weapon and turned to leave.

The beating sobered me up and then I wanted to get high. I just realized I hadn't had a blast in weeks! Not since I got locked up. I remembered the dope I left at the apartment and made my way over there. I just knew both Denise and my dope were in the wind.

Denise sprang from the sofa and rushed me as soon as I walked inside. "Willie!" she sang jumping into my arms. "Oh my God! What happened to your face?"

"I'm cool," I said putting her down, "where my stuff?"

"Right here!" Denise shouted and took off. She returned in a flash with my dope.

"It's all here!" she exclaimed proudly. "Look! All of it! I didn't touch it! Not one bit!"

It looked like what I left her with so I nodded. This was no time for talk. It was time to get high! I loaded a chunk on there big enough to stop a heart and lit it.

"Hmph," I said holding the hit, passing the shooter to Denise.

"That's OK, you go 'head," she declined.

"Hmph!" I demanded with a frown and she took it. I could tell she didn't want to hit it but she did. She looked miserable as she pulled death into her lungs.

After we both hit a few rocks a piece I ordered Denise to strip. I again marveled at how fine the young girl was. I wondered what she could have been if not for drugs —if not for me.

As I pushed inside of her my mind flashed back to the doctor telling me to get tested. In Prentice suicide note she mentioned testing positive, but I didn't care anymore. Besides that still didn't mean I had it. I released weeks of pent up semen and stress inside of Denise and fell asleep on top of her.

~

M y dad caught up with me me on my cell phone a couple of weeks after the funeral. I hadn't been to work or called so I took the call.

"Hey pop!" I said as if all was well, "I know you're wondering when I'm coming to work and—"

"Son, I know what you're doing. Your mother and I can't stop you. If you haven't suffered enough to stop then nothing I can say will stop you."

"So what the fuck you want then? What you call me for?" I demanded.

"Well, your mother wants you out of the condo," he said plainly. "She, um, well we are evicting you."

"Cool. I don't need that shit! Matter fact fuck that condo! Job too. And while we at it fuck you and mom!" I yelled.

I wasn't surprised to see an eviction notice tacked to the front door. According to the date it was served, I was just in time.

Prentice's parents had already retrieved their daughter's belongings, but left Nadirah's for me. I couldn't even bare to open the door to her bedroom. The movers packed up the rest of the house and put it in my storage unit.

I started to ignore Cheryl's call again, as I had for months. Since I had Denise I saw no reason to drive out to her house anymore. She had got the hint and stopped calling for a while, until now.

"Yeah," I answered dryly.

"Oh you don't know me no more huh? She asked with a hint of sarcasm. Wife and daughter got you on lock?"

I snapped inside at the mention of my dead family. "As a matter of fact I need to see you. I got a package I want to give you."

"Well bring it on!" she said seductively.

I stopped by Chubb's and picked up an ounce for us to smoke on. After getting buzzed, I talked my way into her mouth. Cheryl was one of those *don't cum in my mouth* chicks. That always amazed me. What do they expect to happen when they suck a man's dick? Isn't that the purpose? Anyway, when I felt that explosion building I grabbed her head and held it firmly. I pushed all the way in and skeeted on her tonsils.

She squirmed and fought as I filled up her mouth. I held her until she had no choice but to swallow. She took it all down in loud gulps.

"You piece of shit!" she yelled when I finally pulled out. She got up and went to rinse and spit, but I was gone by the time she returned.

I wasn't just content with Cheryl, I made up my mind to spread this misery far and wide.

My next stop was Jewellz foul ass. She was easy to find, still dancing at Club Chocolate. I got her up in the V.I.P. room and let her dance.

"When you gonna let me fuck you?" I announced as she worked her body.

"Nigga you coulda been got this pussy!" she exclaimed.

With that I whipped out my dick. Would you believe this nasty bitch insisted I wear a condom.

"Come on Willie I can't be having no cum running down my leg while I'm on stage," she protested.

I pretended to comply but used my fingernails to tear a hole in the top. I bent her over on the sofa to hit her from the back. The entire head of my dick was sticking out when I slid inside of her.

My intention was to grudge fuck her, but she had some good pussy! Great! Outstanding! I enjoyed slowly long stroking her fine ass. I watched as the rubber rolled back down on my shaft. My dick was shining from her juices and that made me come. I pushed up to the hilt and let her have it.

"Willie! Aww man!" she whined when she turned around and saw the busted rubber. "Now I gotta go douche!"

CHAPTER TWENTY-THREE

I had almost a hundred grand in my account when I quit working and now I was broke. Fucking Prentice made sure I couldn't collect insurance on her by killing herself.

With no source of income and two drug habits to support, something had to give. Something had to go. I started selling off my expensive furniture out of my storage unit. After the big stuff was gone I started selling off my small things.

The pawn shop only paid a dollar for each CD but I had over a thousand, plus several hundred DVDs. Denise and I smoked that up in a week.

Every time I ran out of dope or money I took it out on Denise. Poor thing got raped and beat on a regular basis. Finally she had enough and ran for her life. She escaped one day while I was in one of my coma-like sleeps.

To make up for her absence I began hitting the clubs again. After fucking just about every dancer in the strip club, I made my rounds through the regular clubs. Every night I took a woman home and had unprotected sex with her.

Young, old, fat, skinny, black, white and even a couple of Mexicans. I felt no remorse at possibly infecting all those women. It was their fault for fucking me.

When Angel flew in to see me, I didn't spare her either. She commented about the now obvious changes in my appearance. I chalked it up to being depressed over losing my family. I made up a story about a car accident and she went for it.

I had to make up another story when she asked me to take her to the graves. I still hadn't been out there yet myself. Finally I got her in one of our world famous sixty nines. She willingly swallowed my poisoned semen the whole weekend.

~

"Look if you're ever short on cash you know I'll...work with you," Chubb said as I scraped together odd bills to pay him.

"Aight man," I shot back wearied by the flirting . Still in need of cash, I pulled off an insurance scam. I sold my Lex to a chop shop for five grand, then reported it stolen.

The insurance shot me a check for the twenty-eight grand book value. I bought myself a nice Honda with the five and intended to smoke the rest.

The party waged on with my new influx of cash. Me and Al were back on the party scene. One night we hit the club and I saw a nice looking older lady seated alone. I was taken aback at how pretty she was and in my staring, I saw her as she discreetly snorted coke in the darkness.

"Hi I'm Will," I said boldly taking a seat at her table equipped with a bottle of bubbly and two glasses. "And you are...?"

"Old enough to be your momma!" She laughed, displaying a set of even pearly whites.

"My aunt maybe but not momma," I said, joining in the laughter.

"Rene," she said, extending a pretty hand.

I was already high and half drunk so I tried her up. "Let's go somewhere, I wanna eat you."

"Oh my!" she exclaimed, then shot me a serious look. "I'm very particular in bed. I like it my way!"

"You can have whatever you like," I sang like that rap tune.

"Sweet!" I proclaimed as we entered her lush midtown condo.

"You can have the tour later," she said pulling her dress off over her head. "I recall you said something about eating me."

Eat her I did. I had old girl screaming like a banshee as I twirled my tongue around her large clit. Shit was so big it felt like I was sucking a little dick!

Rene then pulled me up and sexed me for hours under her strict supervision. She instructed me on what positions to hit and how to hit it.

"Harder, softer, deeper, right there!" She barked her way to multiple orgasms.

"Willie, are you trustworthy?" she asked as we laid out on her circular bed.

"Of course I am." I lied.

"I can show you how to make some money," she said, kissing my chest. "Some real money."

Rene gave me head and explained the hustle of busting fake checks. By the time she got me off I was all in.

I was nervous as hell as I presented my first counterfeit check. I examined it thoroughly and it looked fine to me.

"Thank you Mr. McGuire," the pretty teller smiled as she forked over the $20,000.00 I was allowed to keep $5000.00 but had to turn the rest over to Rene.

She claimed the printer gets half and splits the other half with the person who cashes. It was sweet, but not frequent enough for me.

I only got one check a week and ran through the $5000.00 like water. Being the fucking genius that I was, I devised a plan. On the way to the bank I photocopied a check to get all the info.

On the way back from the bank, I bought a professional printer. That night I played around with the program and produced what I thought was a decent counterfeit.

The next day I took it back to that first teller who flirted so openly with me. She frowned then half smiled at my presence.

"Hello Mr. McGuire," she said dryly.

"Hey yourself cutie," I smiled back. Her eyes widened at the sight of the $60,000.00 check. My dumb ass went for broke.

"One second Mr. McGuire," she said taking the check to the rear. If I had followed that inner voice, the one that signals danger, I would have been fine. I should've run...right then!

I saw the teller point at me to a manager. Still, I waited. Waited until a police officer walked right up behind me.

"Sir, I need you to come with me," he said sternly. The firm grip prevented me from bolting. One he got me outside I was cuffed and taken downtown.

Instead of the county jail, I was diverted to the federal building. I sat inside a small interrogation room for hours before someone finally came to see me.

"William Champion, I'm Agent Gonzalez," the Anglo looking man announced. As he spoke he began laying out a bunch of bogus checks. There were only two that belonged to me and I was about to protest until he placed the accompanying surveillance photos with the check. There I was smiling brightly, accepting cash.

"We know you're a pawn, we want the queen," he said finally sitting.

"I can go free if I help?" I asked desperately.

"Free, no," he said quickly, "you can go but with probation. The offer will not be repeated."

The offer did not have to be repeated. I agreed to set Rene up in exchange for probation. I did fuck her old ass one more good time before we arranged the meet.

Rene had a $20,000.00 check for me and several thousand more. The feds got all that plus different IDs and several names. No telling what all they found when they got a warrant for her condo.

If she is as smart as I know she is, she will give up the printer. Well that's not my problem,...I had enough of my own.

My run was coming to an end and I knew it. I was ready to throw in the towel. I decided to get myself together.

"It's not too late," I advised myself. "Go back to rehab, then get my job back."

"Hey Mom," I said cheerfully when my mother picked up. She didn't reply. I heard her put the phone down, then silence.

"Willie? My dad questioned as he picked up.

"What happened to Mom?" I inquired hotly.

"Son, your mother's not ready to talk," he said contritely. I could hear my mother barking at him from the background.

"Dad I'm back! Ready to get clean," I offered smiling through the phone line.

"Yes dear, but, OK," my father mumbled to his complaining wife. "Look son, I have to go. Your mom is still upset. Listen, we're going to Hilton Head tonight for the weekend. Call me Monday and we'll talk," he said just above a whisper.

"Pussy whipped, henpecked ass nigga!" I shouted at the phone. "Fuck it, I'll just keep getting high then!"

"You know I don't like no shorts!" Chubb said shaking his head. "I already told you we can work something out. You know what I'm saying?"

"Look man, I got a check that I gotta cash in the morning," I lied. "I'll bring it back and cop!"

"Well OK," he said eyeing me. "This one is on me, next time is on you, OK?"

"OK Chubb," I agreed, not knowing what I was agreeing to. What I did know is that I needed some cash. And I knew where to get it!

CHAPTER TWENTY-FOUR

I was shocked to see the spare key was still hidden in a faux rock in my parents' flower bed. Knowing the lay of the place from having grown up there, I made quick work of the burglary.

In under a half hour I was loaded down with a couple grand in cash and tens of thousands in jewelry. Now see, I would have spared them and only taken that. When I saw that all traces of me had been removed I got hot. Rage was more like it.

My first thought was to trash the place. Just as I lifted a vase above my head to smash, a better plan came to mind. I rushed out and got a moving truck and cleaned the place out.

I hired a few junkies to help load it and I took everything. What I couldn't sell, pawn or trade for drugs, I gave away. Using the keys hanging in the kitchen I took my mother's new Lexus as well as Dad's vintage Corvette. They needed to be punished for treating me like that. It was their fault I started getting high anyway!

It took all weekend but I got everything but the kitchen sink. And that was only because I didn't have the right tools.

I sold all that shit – cars, pictures, everything. I paid Chubb what I owed him. Faggot looked disappointed when I pulled out all that cash.

Ain't nothing changed. When I get high, I like to fuck. After I copped from Chubb I hit Glenwood looking for a nice smoker to sexually abuse. I had to pass on most of the scrawny stragglers I saw. I still had standards. The bar had certainly been lowered, but standards none the less.

They say lightning doesn't strike twice in the same place and I say they a damn lie! There was Denise at the same pay phone, at the same gas station I met her at the first time. She gained all the weight back that she had lost fucking with me. Her face and eyes were bright and I was hard.

"Hey stranger I said pulling up beside her. "Long time no see."

Denise looked like she wanted to bolt when she saw me. "Oh hey Willie, I don't smoke no more," she said fearfully.

"Well I don't either, well besides weed," I lied. "Anybody got some green out here?"

"Um yeah Rico dem got some fire," she said pointing at a young dred.

"Here, go get us like ten bags," I said stretching a hundred dollar bill towards her. Rico must have had some fire for real the way she moved. "Come on and smoke one."

"I, I...just weed? You ain't gonna hurt me?" she said fearfully.

"Of course not!" I exclaimed. "Let's get something to eat and smoke a few blunts."

The promise of food and weed was enough to get the hood rat in the car. I could tell she wanted to fuck once the shrimp platter was placed in front of her.

When we got back to the apartment we smoked a nice fat blunt and chilled. Once the blunt was done I moved on her. I even ate her salty little pussy, trying to seduce her ass.

It felt like old times sliding back inside Denise. We tongue kissed as we made love for the first time ever. We both got a good nut and drifted off to sleep. Of course I didn't sleep long. I needed a hit.

Denise must have smelled the dope cuz as soon as I pulled it out she woke up. She looked horrified at the sight. I fixed up a nice hit as she watched in awe.

She inhaled along with me as I took a long slow pull of the sizzling drug. I purposely exhaled in her direction and she inhaled it. I stopped short of offering her the smoking pipe.

I wanted it to be her choice. She had to want to smoke it.

"Hey baby I gotta run out for a sec," I said placing the plate containing the rocks and pipe on the night stand beside her. "You need anything while I'm out?"

"I said," I began to repeat myself in an attempt to break the trance the drugs had her in, "I said do you need anything?"

"No I'm fine," she answered to the drug.

I walked over to the gas station for beer and more cigars. I took my sweet time allowing Denise enough time to wrestle with herself.

She lost! When I walked back in the apartment I could hear her pulling from the front room. A smile spread across my face as I walked into the room.

"Welcome home sugar," I said sitting beside her. She nodded and took another hit. As soon as she blew the smoke out I stood in front of her with my hands on my hips. I wanted to see if she remembered her training...if she was still my sex slave.

She pulled my zipper down, pulled out my growing erection and gave the head a loving kiss before taking it deep into her hot mouth.

I knew I had a warrant on me from robbing my parents' house, but I flew under the radar. Denise and I smoked off that money until it was almost depleted.

She suggested we buy enough to flip so we could smoke for free. I would re-up from Chubb and hit the motels. Business was great. It got to the point where we would grind on the weekends and chill during the week.

Business was booming. Sometimes I wouldn't even get time to take a blast. I would buy four ounces, sell three and take one home. I eventually slipped back into my sadistic ways, raping Denise from time to time. I don't even know why I did the shit. The girl would fuck me sideways if I wanted.

She got my ass back good one time. I had just bought four ounces from Chubb. I only had half the money and promised to bring the rest in the morning.

"Here, get the room, I'm gonna run this to the house," I said, giving Denise the money for the room and three of the four ounces.

Man, I got back and ole girl was nowhere to be found. I searched and waited for hours before I admitted to myself that she got me. I went home driving on an empty tank to retrieve the ounce I put up for personal use.

It took more discipline that I thought I had to sell it all. I could only steal small bumps here and there but in the morning I had what I owed Chubb.

"Here you go. Just like I promised," I said proudly handing Chubb his money. "Check I'ma need you to front me a couple ounces to get back on my feet."

"Hmmp," he said turning up his nose as he counted the money. "I can't give you no more credit Willie."

"Why? I paid you! I always pay," I pleaded. I had done right by him and sold that shit instead of smoking it all. He owed me for that.

"Shit you won't never do nothing for me," he replied sounding salty. Like a woman.

"Yes I will. Just name it," I said desperately. I desperately needed a hit. I was down for almost anything. Or so I thought.

"Let me suck your dick," he announced suddenly

"Dude, I don't get down on no gay shit!" I exclaimed hotly.

"OK so don't! Take your business elsewhere or come back when your money is straight," he shot back.

I really don't remember saying yes but I must have because Chubb smiled and knelt down in front of me.

"Oh yeah," he exclaimed when he pulled my limp dick from my pants.

I tensed up and grimaced as he put it in his mouth and began blowing me. I was disgusted by the masculine moans.

"Look, I'ma just stop," Chubb complained after I still couldn't get hard. "I was gonna *give* you an ounce but you acting all funny!"

"OK, OK, try again!" I said thrusting my limp penis at him. This time I tuned out the manly grunts and closed my eyes.

I pretended to be back at Bret's house so many years ago. I'm inside Mel's mouth getting my first blow job ever. It did the trick and I was able to get an erection. A few minutes later Chubb swallowed with a loud disgusting gulp.

"See! That ain't kill you did it?" Chubb laughed as he got up. He bought me out an ounce and pressed it into my hand. "We can do this again you know."

I didn't reply, just left with my dope. The plan was to go flip it and buy the next one. Only problem was I fucked around and smoked most of that shit, then tricked off with some as well. I had to go back to see Chubb again empty handed. Well almost.

The arrangement worked well for a week or so until Chubb put some shit in the game.

"If you still want the blow you gonna have to do something for me," he demanded all fussy like a small girl.

"OK," I said preparing to whip my dick out. I didn't like it but had begun to get used to it. Even got to the point of getting hard instantly.

"I want you to do me one time," he said crossing his legs.

"Do you what?" I shot back. I thought the nigga wanted me to fuck him, As bad as that thought was, what he wanted was worse.

"Un uh, I want some head too. We can sixty nine or take turns," he offered.

Man I ain't sucking your dick!" I yelled as a rage began to slowly boil.

"Then go! Get out!" He demanded. "You're a taker! It's all about you!"

I wanted to leave but couldn't. I wanted to get high. I needed to, had to. My life depended on it. I sank down into the chair defeated but at the same time trying to contain the simmering rage.

Chubb misunderstood my sitting as approval and approached. I felt like I was turning green, about to bust out my clothes. He held the back of my head and pushed his dick towards my face. When I felt it brush against my cheek I lost it.

"You think I'm a faggot!" I screamed, leaping from the chair. I beat Chubb with both hands until he fell. He tried to crawl away as I kicked and stomped him.

Finally I dove on his back and began choking him. He clawed at my hands and arms, drawing blood in a futile attempt to save his life.

"Whose the faggot now nigga!" I asked repeatedly as I choked the life out of Chubb. Even when he stopped kicking and clawing, I kept on squeezing. Finally the rage began to ebb and I got up.

"Where the dope at homie?" I chuckled at his prone body. I knew it was in the room to the left from all the times I'd copped over the years.

"Jackpot," I laughed as I found neatly packaged ounces of crack and powdered cocaine. Next to the dope was thousands of dollars in cash. I scooped all of it up, along with jewelry and other valuables I found laying around, including my dad's Rolex from Chubb's dead wrist.

~

I ditched my downtown apartment in favor of the rundown hotels. That was where the action was. I partied and tricked nonstop.

That was when I started feeling sick. Everyday it seemed like I lost a few more pounds. Everyday I felt a little weaker...a little sicker. Still, I continued drinking, smoking and fucking.

Crack whores would wait turns to come smoke and fuck. Wouldn't you know it? Why'd Denise show up at my door? It was a worn out, war torn version of the pretty young girl but it was her. We had both changed so drastically that we didn't recognize each other until she was in and seated.

"Well, well, well, look what the cat dragged in," I slurred.

"Willie?" she said puzzled at my new appearance.

"Yeah, it's me," I laughed. Word around the hotels was that I was a trick, so junky whores made it their business to come get high for free, then they were subjected to my sicknesses—literally. "I missed you."

"Um, I missed you too," she lied. I knew she was scared but the promise of free dope kept her in place.

"You know I got locked up that night. The police stopped me and found the dope," she lied.

I could tell from her ragged appearance that she smoked all of it, every crumb. By herself!

"You ain't mad?" she asked trying to be seductive but in her emaciated state it was kind of creepy.

"Of course not," I exclaimed. "Matter fact I really missed you! Come over here."

Denise hesitated for a second, then came and joined me on the bed. She accepted the outstretched shooter and put it to her lips. I stood up just as she flicked the lighter.

My rage consumed me as I watched her take a greedy pull on the pipe. I threw a hard right that even with my weakened state knocked her out cold. I jumped on the bed and tore her clothes off her frail body.

Denise woke with a shrill scream when I penetrated her anus. She was thrashing and screaming so much that I had to shove her face into the pillow to mute it. I kept up the pressure until she fell limp...died actually. Since I had yet to climax I continued sodomizing her until I came.

The rape took everything else that I had in me. It was as if my life skeeted into her dead body. I was so exhausted I curled up next to the corpse and went to sleep. A sleep so deep I was surprised to awake the next day.

I was dead on my feet. A force beyond anything I could explain propelled me to my destination. I fell asleep on the bus but awoke mysteriously at my transfer point. The same thing happened when I reached my destination. My eyes popped open just in time.

A coughing fit wracked my body taking more life with every hack. I knew it was more irony or coincidence that on the anniversary of my wife's death I was staggering towards her grave.

Although I'd never been there, my soul directed me to the spot where both my child and wife were buried. I noticed that the names on the tombstones didn't mention Champion. Nadirah and Prentice Willowby shared a grave.

It took my absolute last step to make it to their graves. I collapsed on top of them and closed my eyes. Then, I began to rise. They say your life flashes before your eyes at death and it does. I saw every failure, every let down as I rose. My mind shot to the incident at the pool so many years before.

Only this time, my father couldn't save me. No one or nothing could help me now. Higher and higher, I drifted away from my body. I smiled realizing I would not be going back. It was over, it was...

The End

EPILOGUE

"Yes, how can I help you?" My mother asked the officer as she answered her door.

Mrs. Champion?" He asked checking the name and address on his pad. "Is Mr. Champion here as well?"

"Yes, one second. William!" She called, summoning my dad.

"Yes Sessalie?" He came quickly hearing distress in her voice. "Officer?"

"Um yes, well I'm sorry to have to inform you but we found a body. It was at a grave, and um it, well he, was identified as William Champion Jr. I'm sorry to tell you that your son has died," he said painfully.

"There must be some mistake, officer. Our son died years ago," she said as she closed the door.

www.ingramcontent.com/pod-product-compliance
Lightning Source LLC
Chambersburg PA
CBHW060435180626
46817CB00007B/2825